Praise For
Murder Squared
a Kate Cooper Mystery

"Suspenseful southern thriller with old money and a serial murderer in play. Our main character is a tenacious reporter who has moved from DC to Savannah and is investigating a string of murders with bodies dumped in well known city squares, all while struggling with caring for her ailing mother, navigating the politics of asking questions about powerful Savannah families, and her own relationship. This book is full of intrigue and sprinkled with fun historical facts that have you going 'wait really?' all throughout."

— Bridget Zatezalo, *Tucker, Georgia*

"Dynamic characters and an original plot make Murder Squared a riveting page-turner that I did not want to put down. I thoroughly enjoyed the history intertwined with suspense and look forward to visiting the squares mentioned in the book to immerse myself more in the characters' thoughts and actions."

— Lauren Greene, *Savannah, Georgia*

"I read ahead to see who did it, then went back and read it again... As a former Savannah resident, I loved the way the squares were intertwined with the story."

— Glynda Caddell, *West Palm Beach, Florida*

"Intriguing mystery novel that effortlessly weaved historical information about the host city, Savannah, GA, into the story. I was kept in suspense until the very end and learned more about a city I've had the pleasure of visiting many times."

— Katie Zummo, *Springfield, Virgina*

Murder Squared

a Kate Cooper Mystery

by Rome Collier

Cover Design: Lauren Clackum

Paperback ISBN: 978-1-959563-13-6
eBook ISBN: 978-1-959563-14-3

Published by:
Maudlin Pond Press
P.O. Box 53
Tybee Island, GA 31328
www.maudlinpond.com

To Geni, the source of all the magic

1. Franklin Square

The streetlight at the corner of Franklin Square cast an orange glow on the paving bricks and contrasting streaks of darkness through the live oaks surrounding the plaza. The shadows fell heaviest on the Haitian monument at the center of the square, where bronze soldiers stood frozen like players on a stage, memorializing heroes who traveled hundreds of miles from their Caribbean island home to fight with American colonists in their revolution against an empire.

There was a stillness and a chill in the early morning air. Fog that settled on Savannah's streets during the night had risen into a fine mist enshrouding the treetops and steeples of the old Southern seaport city. Across the street from the square, the Old City Market was quiet, now hours after the last restaurants and shops had closed.

At first glance, the corpse at the foot of the monument appeared as if it might have been a statue fallen from the platform where the other figures were poised to help try to retake Savannah from the British in 1779. But this corpse was real.

The body was covered but not bagged by the time Kate arrived. It was 4 a.m. on a Sunday, and normally she would not be here. But this was the third one – the third victim found murdered and dumped in one of the characteristic squares which followed Savannah's original 18th century design.

Three in nine months was a clear sign of a serial killer. That was enough to get any earnest crime reporter going even in the middle of the night on a weekend. She grinned inwardly at the thought of herself as being a "crime reporter" back in her hometown. It was a long way from the nation's capital, where her journalistic career started.

Kate parked around the corner in front of a police car blinking blue and red and walked about 50 yards back to the crime scene. She arrived at the square thinking about how this latest victim confirmed a hunch she had after the second one was found folded into a sitting position beside the gazebo at Crawford Square on the edge of the Historic District just before Thanksgiving.

That poor woman had been poisoned. The first guy was stabbed – literally in the back – before he was discovered stripped naked and stuffed into a black plastic garbage bag in Oglethorpe Square one fair May Day morning.

That meant the primary link between the killings of these two retirees, who both came from families of considerable means, was the unusual circumstance in which their bodies were found. Kate was aware that a lot hinged on details of this latest victim, especially identity and cause of death.

A garbage truck clanged in the alley, removing remains from Saturday night feasts in fancy restaurants, as she stepped over the curb and spied Detective Sergeant Rod Armstrong. He saw her coming.

“Kate Cooper, cub reporter. I’m surprised to see you here. You here to get a scoop, Coop?”

“No. I just like going out in the middle of the night to talk to dimwitted detectives. What do we have here?”

Actually, she’d had a pretty good rapport with Armstrong since switching to the police beat the preceding year. He was honest, as far as it went, and usually told her what he could, even if she sometimes had to keep it under wraps. But verbal jousting with these guys was necessary, in the squad room and the street, to maintain proper respect.

“I forget. Do you prefer Detective Armstrong or Sergeant Armstrong?” she said, taking out a pen and a small pad from her belt pack, pretending to make a note of his name. (She normally taped notes on her phone.)

"I prefer Detective Sergeant Armstrong! But you can call me the man who stands between you and the story you crawled out of bed to get at four in the morning." His six-foot frame literally blocked her view of the shrouded corpse, stood over by a pot-bellied uniformed officer and a lab technician wearing navy scrubs.

Crime scene investigators were scurrying about for anything out of the ordinary, other than Exhibit No. 1 at the base of the monument. A pair of them were over at the First African Baptist Church on the opposite corner from the Market.

"What can you tell me?" she asked as Armstrong turned to the side and extended his arm to usher her closer to the center of action. They stepped nearer to the body, still 25 to 30 feet away.

"You might as well have stayed in bed. We have nothing at this point. White male, appears to be in his late 60s. Cause of death undetermined at this point."

"How do you know that it's homicide?"

He cocked his head in feigned surprise. "We don't. That's being investigated, too."

"Well, you're here. That's good enough for me." Armstrong was one of the top investigators.

"Sergeant, can you come here for a minute, please." Another detective – Wills, Kate was thinking his name was – was kneeling by the victim.

"Wait right here." Armstrong stepped over to where the corpse lay. The other detective appeared to point somewhere toward the neck area. Other than that, all Kate could see was the back of a head, with short cropped silver hair. She couldn't make out what the two men were saying.

Another blue-garbed technician started helping the first one begin bagging the body as Armstrong moved back over to Kate.

"As I was saying, the mere fact that you're here qualifies it as homicide. In fact, under the circumstances it looks like it's one of a serial."

"And, as I was saying, you wasted your time coming out here. There will be a press briefing at 9 a.m. at police headquarters. Until then nothing more will be disclosed other than what I've told you. That much will be contained in the announcement of the press briefing, which will come out in a few minutes, so your paper will then know everything you know now. Does that make sense?"

Kate noticed that the body bag was being placed into the back of a van backed up to the Haitian memorial.

"Excuse me." She stepped to the side of Armstrong and took a photo with her phone. "Well, that's one thing we couldn't get from a press release. That and the color of the scene."

Armstrong allowed her to look around while his men began wrapping up the most intense part of their crime scene investigation. By now, the plaza appeared placid, with everything in place. Kate took a few more shots of the monument and the detectives at the church.

"Who found the body?" Kate asked.

"A worker at a nearby restaurant, cutting through the park."

"Name?"

"Ha! Fat chance!"

"How did somebody get the body in here without being seen? Surely, they would have been picked up on some sort of security camera, anyway."

Armstrong sighed.

"All under investigation, Miss Cooper." He gestured toward his watch as he turned to go. "Nine a.m.!"

Kate took a couple more pictures of the scene and walked hurriedly back to her car. There were some things she could write that spoke for themselves. That would hold it until the news conference. All the TV stations would have the news about the body being found as soon as they got the press release.

At least The Tide, the startup online news outlet that paid her bills, would be first. She could write a few paragraphs for the website, update it as soon as she could learn the identity of the dead man, and then fill it in with as much as she could get from the news conference.

It only took a couple of minutes to file her photos and a brief story:

> "BODY FOUND IN CITY SQUARE
>
> "Third in nine months
>
> "A man was found dead in Franklin Square early Sunday, just a few months after two other bodies were found in city squares. Police are investigating whether the latest is related to the first two deaths.
>
> "The cause of death of the latest victim, a white male believed to be in his mid to late 60s, had not been determined just after the body was found about 3 a.m. by a restaurant worker. Police say a briefing will be held at headquarters about 9 a.m., at which time other details might be revealed.
>
> "Nancy Janston Oliver, 67, was found dead in Crawford Square just before Thanksgiving, a victim of antifreeze poisoning. Max Long, 73, was stabbed to death and his body left in a garbage bag in Oglethorpe Square last May Day. Those deaths are still under investigation, along with disposal of the victims."

Now all she had to do was wait a few hours until the news conference. The good thing was it gave her an excuse to see Paul. She hadn't seen him for four or five days, ever since he took umbrage – once again – at one of her many suggestions that he may be lacking in ambition. In recent text exchanges he still seemed distant— the only guy she'd known who could seem more distant than a text.

Kate could think of nothing better than to cozy up and cuddle away those bruised feelings.

2. Kate and Paul

"Hello, baby!"

The voice on his phone was smooth and sweet, but for Paul Camden it was not a smooth awakening.

"Huh... what... Kate?... What time is it?"

She gave him a few seconds. "It's almost 5 a.m."

"I'm sitting outside. Have to kill a few hours before a police news conference about a murder. Buzz me up."

It took another beat or two for things to sink in. "My buzzer is broken. I'll come down."

By the time Kate gathered her laptop, phone and purse and climbed the steps to the four-story apartment building Paul was at the door, dressed in a pink terry cloth robe she had left there months earlier.

"What on Earth..." she laughed as she brushed by, tugging gently on the ridiculously short sleeve, which came almost to his elbow. She gave him a gentle kiss on the mouth and stepped into the tiny elevator. Didn't detect any booze on his breath, so that was a good thing.

"So, what's the deal again? You say the cops are having a press briefing on a murder?"

He punched four and the lift jerked into its ascent.

"That's right. Another body was found in a park. This time Franklin Square. Different MO, similar means of disposal. Could be a serial thing."

"Could be a copycat thing. Could be anything," he said. By now they were inside his one-bedroom flat overlooking Forsyth Park. "What do the cops say?"

"No comment. Armstrong, anyway. He was there."

Paul smirked. "Armstrong. What a dick."

"He's OK. Can be obnoxious at times. He doesn't care much for you, either, though," she said as she climbed into the four-poster bed wearing only a light sweater and panties. "What's the matter with your buzzer, anyway?"

"I don't know. The super's supposed to fix it Monday. It's only been out a couple of days."

Paul crawled into the bed beside her, and she snuggled close. She immediately felt his hand on her thigh.

"I don't know what you're thinking, but whatever it is that's not why I'm here."

He yawned a sigh.

"It was a late night for me, too, and I've got a tour and have to be at the Visitor's Center at 10."

He reached over and turned off the lamp on the nightstand.

"You're not still mad about last week?" Kate said.

"Well, hurt, anyway." He kissed her gently. Then, feeling forgiven, she rolled over and they slept, still a couple of hours to go before daylight.

Paul was the main reason Kate didn't regret her decision to move back to Savannah to take care of her mother after her stroke. She grew up in the city, the daughter of a self-described "simple redneck" from nearby Hardeeville, S.C., and a Guamanian mother whose own father was a Black American sailor from Brooklyn. Kate and her parents had lived around various Air Force bases until she was 9 years old, and her dad retired from the service and settled back closer to home, working at the International Paper mill until he died of a heart attack at 54.

At the time Kate was in her sophomore year at the University of Georgia. She went to UGA to study computers but got caught up in working for The Red & Black student newspaper and switched to journalism. Master's studies at American University in Washington led to an internship at a D.C. television station, and that to a digital editing job at The Washington Post, where she toiled for several years before getting a crack as a metro reporter at the Washington Times.

It was work she loved. She was on the verge of covering politics in the nation's capital when her mother, Katherine, got sick. With no one else to take care of her, Kate took the plunge and moved into her mom's house on Wilmington Island.

Journalism jobs were in short supply, especially in a city the size of Savannah. Her experience, coupled with willingness to work for peanuts, got her hired at The Tide, a mostly online startup that printed just enough editions to sell almost as souvenirs from hotels and racks along River Street and other heavy tourist areas.

At first, she wrote a column about various sites of interest to visitors and Savannah residents alike. That's how she met Paul – or rather, got reacquainted with him. He was a guide on trolley tours of the city, and a wealth of information. They had known each other at Savannah High but never dated or anything, even though she always had a crush on him.

And he on her, as it turned out. Kate was legendary in high school for her golden complexion, black hair, and exotic Micronesian eyes.

Paul was the one who suggested she start a police beat at The Tide. He had been a cop himself, after four years in the Marines and a history degree at Georgia Southern University. He was disillusioned by racial and economic prejudice in the judicial system, as well as by endemic corruption that he felt sworn to do something about.

As a cop, you rely on the word you get on the streets. And when the same people who are giving you information about crime in their streets are also talking about crime in high places you have to take it seriously.

He made the mistake of trying to investigate things by himself rather than passing the information on to superiors. Trying to prove colleagues were protecting a drug dealer, Paul was arrested while arranging a deal involving 100 pounds of marijuana. Not buying or selling himself, mind you; just making a couple of phone calls.

Somebody was sending him a message. And they held all the cards. To fight it would have meant the possibility of a long time behind bars. He pleaded guilty in exchange for his badge and just 10 months in prison.

He lived simply in his small apartment, worked hard conducting tours and researching history. He didn't have a lot of trust in people, but to those he trusted he was a good friend.

And to complete the image of the hard-luck ex-Marine he had an antique Harley Davidson Sportster that was in constant disrepair and which he was always trying to fix.

Except for those who knew him well, Paul was a pariah at the police department. Still, he knew what was going on both within the police and throughout the city. As he explained to Kate, street crime was on the rise, and it was important to delve behind sensational headlines and explore the causes and effects among the people who were closest to it. In the long run, he believed understanding just might enable leaders to make decisions that could lead to solutions.

Her editor was reluctant, thinking that more stories about crime would be bad for the hospitality trade, The Tide's primary source of advertising. But after a trial run of a few weeks, web traffic increased among viewers who lived in Savannah fulltime, a sign they were getting content that they found informative and useful. That increase came without any loss of circulation in hard copies.

Now there was something that would provide a real test of the taste for crime news: a serial killing.

3. Serial Killer

"At this point you can't call it that!"

Paul was a stickler for evidentiary procedure. Kate, sitting and sipping coffee by the bay window that formed one corner of his bedroom, understood the definition of serial killer but wasn't buying it.

"Oh, come on! You have three people murdered, and their bodies are found dumped in three different city squares and you can't conclude it's a serial killing?"

"First of all, no one wants a serial killer in the city a few weeks before St. Patrick's festivities, the biggest deal of the year. Therefore, the cops don't want one either," he said.

"You won't get them to say it officially if a body turns up every day until then," Paul laughed.

"Well, thank God for a free press," Kate countered.

"Now, if the cause of death of the third one is definitely homicide, the cops will agree that they are targeted, but the hallmark of a serial killer is some sort of pattern in respect to motive and/or method, and until that pattern emerges – or the killer makes himself known in some way – we're left with other possibilities."

By now, he was moving into the bathroom to brush his teeth. She took the last drops of coffee and stepped toward the kitchen to put her mug in the sink.

"Well, we'll see what the cops come up with. It's almost quarter 'til. I'd better scoot."

"I'm just asking: Do we have a serial killer – acting out some fantasy rooted God knows where – or a spree killer, choosing victims for a reason and maybe even wrapping up his business after just two or three?"

To Kate, that seemed like splitting hairs, but she would let it go. She had learned that he sometimes didn't like to be disagreed with, a trait she found distasteful and didn't understand. After all, she doubted herself at times; why not doubt the conclusions of someone you happen to love?

As she took her purse and laptop from the foot of the bed, he grabbed her forearm and pulled her toward him. His kiss tasted of mint, but it made her feel that he was glad she had stopped by.

"I'll see you later," she said. "What are you doing for lunch?"

"I will be at Clary's, but not until after two."

"Then I'll catch up with you later. After the news conference, I'm running out to mom's to get her up and something to eat. Then I'll probably try to get some more sleep."

"Maybe we can have dinner tonight?"

"I'll call you."

She left the apartment and trotted down the staircase rather than wait for the rickety elevator. Police headquarters was just about five minutes away through the heart of downtown.

Savannah was settled by English colonists led by General James Oglethorpe in 1733 along a high bluff overlooking the river that shares its name and forms the border between Georgia and South Carolina. The settlement's design consisted of blocks of land called wards with a common area – a plaza, or square – in the center. Each square was surrounded by residential lots, with "trust" lots at the corners reserved for churches, markets, or other public buildings.

Initially, there were four squares. The city expanded over a century or so to include twenty-four before vastly overreaching the area that could accommodate the design. At first they were not the shady and grassy parklike enclaves of today, with huge live oaks draped with Spanish moss. Mostly, they were sandy lots, common areas that could be used for public gatherings of all sorts.

Those along Bull Street, running between the Savannah River and Forsyth Park to the south, were meant for grand events. Some bear statues or memorials to dignitaries and war heroes, such as Oglethorpe or Revolutionary War Gen. Nathaniel Greene.

Today, most are adorned with magnolias and oaks, camellia and azaleas which blossom in various reds, pinks and white, and gardenia that casts its magical scent each spring and early summer. From a grand fountain at Johnson Square to a basketball court at another, each retains some unique characteristics.

Four were lost to the city's development over time, but two have been restored, leaving a total of twenty-two. Kate took a route past four of them on her way from Paul's apartment, at the northwest corner of Forsyth Park, to police headquarters on Oglethorpe Avenue. She was trying to imagine what would lead someone to murder people and leave their bodies in the parks. Why those victims; why thouse parks?

The radio wasn't trying to make sense of it. As she arrived, all-news station WSVK was blaring about a "serial killer on the loose."

"More details of this horrific crime are just minutes away," intoned Todd Worlick, who to Kate was more annoying in person than he was on the air. She parked in the vacant lot across Habersham from police headquarters.

Inside, she saw TV lights set up in a conference room and noticed several other of her competitors from the Morning News and at least three of the local stations. The turnout wasn't as big as you'd expect for a story of this magnitude, but it was a Sunday morning, after all.

The police spokeswoman, Martha Orlando, introduced Lt. Michael Long, chief of detectives, and said he would make a brief statement, followed by questions. Sergeant Armstrong stood at Long's side.

"Let me begin by saying that we have identified the homicide victim whose body was discovered about 3:30 a.m. this morning at Franklin Square. He is 68-year-old Frederick Wallace Pederall III, of Savannah, a retired investor living on a pension.

"Because of the unusual circumstances regarding disposal of the victim, and similarities to two other homicides within the past year, we regard these to be targeted killings. The relationship between the three is under investigation, and at this time the motive of the perpetrator – or perpetrators – is not known."

"Cause of death of Pederall?" Worlick shot out from the back of the room.

"He was killed by a sharp object, probably an ice pick, penetrating the brain from the back of his head. He was already unconscious at the time of death. Toxicology tests are under way to find out why."

"Just a reminder," Orlando interjected, "questions will follow the lieutenant's remarks."

"That's alright," Long said. "As I said, everything is under investigation. We just want to underscore that we believe the general public is safe. There is reason to believe that whoever did this has selected certain individuals."

"Does Pederall have a family?" asked Doris Good from the Morning News.

"He lived alone, like the first two. There is a stepdaughter from a second marriage. She lives on Hilton Head and has been notified." Long nodded to Kate, who had held up her hand to be recognized.

"Have surveillance cameras provided no leads?"

Worlick interrupted before the detective could answer. "Do you have any suspects?"

"The answer to both questions is 'no comment.' I've given you the results of our investigation so far, this early in the process. Let me say, though, that cameras in public domains are not a panacea for solving crime. But we are making use of whatever resources that are available to solve these crimes."

"Franklin Square, isn't that the one with the Haitians?" someone asked.

"That's right. The drummer boy who later became king of Haiti and all that," Long said. "At the west end of City Market."

As usual at one of these briefings, it broke down into each of the reporters asking pretty much the same question in a different way and getting the same response: "That aspect is under investigation." They all went over the same general questions two or three times, with no new information forthcoming except for one detail: There was no sign of forced entry at Pederall's apartment, just as in the case of the first two victims.

Kate sidled over to Armstrong.

"Looks like the city is safe as long as you're not a senior with friends you can't trust," she offered.

"Right now, I'd give anything if it was that simple. Just don't go around putting everybody on edge. Strictly off the record because I'm not supposed to talk to you about it, but there's no reason to think some psychopathic killer is out there, picking people at random to murder. That'll do nothing but create panic."

"Oh yeah, I'm sure whoever is doing this is perfectly sane."

"The point is, from a public safety standpoint and from the standpoint of our investigation, there is a distinction. You do your work, and we'll do ours. Just don't write things that make it more difficult for us, OK?"

"Alright, you've got a deal."

4. The Screven Arms

Kate updated her story with the identity of the dead man and the suspected cause of death, emphasizing the targeted victim's age and the fact that there was no forced entry at his or the other victims' homes. She still saw no reason to actually use the term "serial killer" or "serial killing." The facts spoke for themselves: three dead under very mysterious circumstances, their bodies placed in the parks.

She got the address of the latest victim, Pederall, from Armstrong and set out to see if she could find any neighbors or grieving family who might talk to her about him. It was a modern high-rise called the Screven Arms on Drayton Street between Oglethorpe and Broughton Streets. The apartment had been sealed by police. She rang a few doorbells, but none answered, and there was no one in the hallway, which was surprisingly dimly lit.

It was the same in the lobby, which was tropically themed down to aquariums with colorful fish along the walls. "Odd," Kate thought. "It's as though no one lives in this entire 12-story building."

She was peering into her phone to see what others were reporting and was surprised to run into Howell Barker about to enter as she stepped out onto the sidewalk. Howell was a local history buff and a friend of Paul's. However, compared to Paul he was one of the green eyeshade types who delved deep into birth records, deeds, and wills dating back centuries as they traced Savannah's sometimes decaying roots into the past.

Mercilessly tormented as "Howler Barker" as a kid, Howell had turned inward to academics at an early age.

"Hi, Howell. What are you doing here?"

She startled him. His habit was to look not at eye level but straight ahead, which was disconcerting when talking to him while peering down at his 5-foot-3 frame. He was a grown man in his 40s but looked like a child.

"Oh, hi Kate." Stopping in midtrack, gazing somewhere off her left shoulder. It was not as bad as when he looked up at her, with eyes like a wounded puppy. "I'm here to visit my aunt. She lives up on the fourth floor, down the hall from Mr. Pederall. I guess that's what brings you here."

"Well, yeah. I was hoping to talk to somebody, but this place is like a tomb."

"They're all afraid, I'm sure. I know Aunt May wouldn't open her door to anyone right now. I have my own key because I come almost every day."

"I just hit a couple of buzzers by the door, and somebody let me into the lobby. Maybe they're expecting someone. Or maybe they don't care as long as they don't open their own door," Kate said.

"And maybe that's how the killer got in! Overall, it's probably better not to expose yourself to strangers, especially now," Howell offered.

"Yes," Kate said. "Did you know Mr. Pederall?"

Howell glanced nervously at the fish tank. And the fish seemed to look nervously at him.

"Never met the man. Know very little about him. I think his family was from Savannah, too." He sensed that she was about to ask him about his aunt. "Aunt May didn't know him, either. Saw him in the building a few times, that's all. Apparently, he kept pretty much to himself – as she does, and practically everybody in the building."

"Well, that alone is helpful, Howell. Good seeing you."

"Take care, Kate." He punched a code and was about to enter the lobby as she turned toward her car parked by the curb, then stopped suddenly.

"Oh, Howell?" He halted in the doorway. "Have you talked to Paul about this? About any of the killings. Now that it's three..."

"Well, gee, Kate, no. The first two... I mean it's hard to think much of something like that these days. And we just found out about the other one. Why?"

"Don't you think it's strange that these murder victims were all of about the same age. I mean, retired, and very similar social status. Do you suppose there's any connection related to that?"

"Well, I don't know, Kate. I'll talk to Paul if you think it'll help. See if we can come up with anything."

"Good. Give him a call. He gets off at two. Said he would be having lunch at Clary's."

She got in her car and drove to her mother's. The Tide was way ahead on the story. After all, it was first. You can't get much better than that in the news business – as long as it's right in the end. That's why it was important not to get ahead of herself. "Let the police investigate, and the rest will take care of itself." It was probably better not to aggravate them. More likely to get information, anyway.

Kate took East Bay to President Street and the Islands Expressway. Wilmington Island is the most populated of the sea islands and hammocks dispersed among the myriad marshes, rivers, and estuaries east of Savannah. U.S. 80, once a major east-west route from California, terminates at Tybee Island, a beach resort town where the Savannah River empties into the Atlantic.

Kate's mother lived just off the highway in a subdivision a couple of blocks from Johnny Mercer Boulevard, the other major route cutting through the island communities. Her parents had lived in the three-bedroom block-and-stucco home for two years, and she was in her sophomore year at UGA, when her dad died.

Things were OK for her mom for a few years until she had a series of strokes, ranging in severity to the one that almost killed her two years ago. Only then, though, had Katherine declined to the point where Kate felt compelled to move her to a nursing home. If this serial killing had not emerged, she quite likely would be preoccupied now trying to place her.

As it was, she felt lucky to have Barbara next door. A retired nurse, she would continue to stay with her mom – for a couple of nights, anyway. She called on her all the time for day duty. Her mother had a generous Social Security check and the remains of two pensions that would compensate Barbara, who was awake and, in the kitchen when she arrived.

She woke her mother up and changed and washed her. Then she got her up and into the den, where she could be fed while watching television and gaze out into the back garden.

Kate and Barbara made some quick arrangements for the night ahead. Afterwards, she lay down on the veranda in the den and fell asleep.

Barbara rapping on the screen door awakened her three hours later. Her mother dozed in the recliner.

"I didn't realize you would be so busy with this horrible story."

It occurred to Kate that for a woman living alone, and about the same age as the three victims, that it all could hit closer to home.

"Yes, it is horrible. But don't worry. It seems to be a downtown thing so far." She could see the worried look on Barbara's face and put her arms around her.

"Oh, Barbara, I don't know what I would do without you." This brought out the most caring reassurances in a soothing Southern drawl.

"Honey, you know I'd do anything for you and your mom."

She took Highway 80 into town, across the Thunderbolt Bridge to Victory Drive. The old fishing village of Thunderbolt, with century-old homes on a bluff above the Wilmington River, was the last bit of inland high ground before the terrain gave way to a watery expanse of creeks and marsh grass to the east of what comprised the English settlement of Savannah.

Today, Thunderbolt is part of the city, although technically it has its own government and police force, known for strict enforcement of traffic laws. Kate made sure her speed was within the limit as she cruised past the houses and shopping strips, under Truman Parkway and by the Victorian mansions along the palm-lined avenue.

She plopped into a booth across from Paul at Roma Christina, a small eatery they liked in Midtown. He seemed absorbed in his phone, so she checked hers without even saying hello. Still no messages – and no news on the killings. But after all, it was a Sunday in Savannah.

"You know," he said. "I've been on Google all day and it's almost like these folks don't even exist."

"Well, technically, I guess they don't now. They're dead."

He ignored her sarcasm. "I mean, after checking almost every aspect I could find on each of their lives – schools, churches, social clubs, and family connections – I could find only one thing linking all three victims. Two of them might have attended the same church or school, but only one tie connects all three."

She waited for him to go on. A waitress appeared at her side.

Looking up, "Just water, please."

"Well, are you going to tell me or am I going to have to guess."

He peered up from the tiny screen. "The Seraphim Society." The waitress set down a cloth-covered basket of rolls and turned toward the kitchen.

"The Seraphim Society?"

Another of the awkward pauses she was beginning to hate. If he wasn't so good looking, she would have had to dump him long ago.

"Yeah," he said, smiling slightly because he knew his conversational habits irritated her from time to time. "It's a charity spinoff of the Seraphim Corporation, which in the latter part of the 19th century was one of the largest investment holding companies in the Southeast."

Kate began buttering a roll.

"I never heard of it. What does it do now?" She bit into the soft bread, which was still warm.

"Well, it was dissolved gradually over the next 100 years, sold off in bits and pieces, I believe. Today, the only remnant that bears its name is the foundation and trust called the Seraphim Society."

Silence again fell on the table. Kate felt another cue was needed to keep the dialogue going.

"So, what does it do?"

"Interestingly," Paul said, turning off his phone and laying it beside his bread plate, "its only relevant duty, according to the charter, is 'to care for and maintain, in concert with other public and private entities, various public squares of the city of Savannah.'"

5. Society of Angels

The Seraphim Society, of course, provided many other charitable functions – only none having any apparent link to the current string of murders.

"A Seraph, according to Christian tradition, is of the highest order of angel, with a burning passion for doing God's work throughout Creation," Paul explained. "In Kabballah, a mystical discipline of Judaism, they are of the first realm of Creation: divine understanding."

Their server brought their drinks, water for her and a beer for Paul.

"So, what happened? This company just started existing only to help people and then went out of business? I can get the name for a charity organization but fail to see the religious connotation elsewhere."

Paul gently poured the pale amber fluid into his glass, creating a small tuft of foam on top. A tuft like an angel's wing.

"Not exactly. See, there is a religious connection, only not in the way you might think. This corporation, or at least the predecessor companies that composed it, went way back, practically to the city's founding. Some of the earlier settlers, after they got established here, believed they were doing God's work by creating the means to further His plan for the king's colony of Georgia.

"Remember, initially Savannah was not a slave-holding city. That came later. But many of the colonists were debtors or otherwise paying off some obligation to the crown or society.

"They were establishing the roots for growth and prosperity for generations to come, they felt they were assisting the angels. The motto of the colony trustees was "Not for self; but for others."

"This port flourished as settlement continued in the interior, up the river, and farther south on the coast. By the time of the invention of the cotton gin – which occurred on a Georgia plantation very near here in the 1790s – the businessmen who headed these families were very well positioned to make a fortune in the process of bettering Creation."

They ordered then, and Kate began filling Paul in on her mother's condition and the arrangement with Barbara. He agreed there was little else she could do. The topic also quietly settled the question of whether she would be going home with him.

"Paul, do you think the Seraphim Society could have anything to do with the murders?"

He gave it no thought.

"Hard to see how. It could just be a coincidence. These peo ple were all about the same age and had solitary lifestyles. That probably had more to do with them winding up dead than any club they might have joined. My understanding is that by the time the corporation was fully dissolved, membership in the charitable foundation was strictly an honorary position, sort of a birthright to people of a certain generation born into certain families."

"After all these years?"

Paul's face suggested, "Yes, surprising, isn't it?"

"You have to remember," he said, "these families were proud survivors. Some of them go back to the origins of this city, and their legacy includes wars, hurricanes, fires... epidemics. You name the hard times that have afflicted mankind throughout history, and they visited here.

"Of course, over centuries families rise and fall. Some dwindled out. Others spread from intermarriage with other proud people – the Irish, the Germans, Italians, Greeks, and others who came here for many of the same reason as Oglethorpe's colonists. Over time, wealth, power, and influence may have diminished, but not that pride."

"Where did you get all this?"

"From various sources on the Internet, with a couple of pointers from Howell. He told me he saw you today."

Kate couldn't help but smile, thinking of Howell's strange ways.

"Odd guy, that Howell. It's easy to understand how he was picked on as a kid."

"Well, he knows more about Savannah and its secrets than anyone. Except for Frank Miller."

"Who's that?"

"You know him. He sometimes takes my trolley tour, just for old times' sake. It used to be his route. He retired from the tour company long before I came along."

"Oh, yeah. I know who you're talking about." Kate was recalling the face that went with the name. "He seems a lot more professorial than Howell, though."

They fell silent for a moment. Kate sensed he was still holding a grudge from their last "dinner date." She had brought up the subject he least liked to discuss: the future.

It wasn't a rule that you had to be set on a course for life success by your mid-30s. Still, most people by then have some idea of where they're going. With Paul, it was like he had already had that, got derailed, and now had no intention of getting back on track.

They were just different personalities. Kate was comfortable, and involved, in whatever group she found herself in. Paul was aloof, and blunt in conversation in a manner that some found off-putting. She had to admit that she herself had no idea of what he could be doing that would make him any better than he was now. The future would unfold, rest assured.

She wasn't looking for marriage, but he was the first guy she had known that she honestly felt she could live with the rest of her life – or would want to. As for family, kids, she thought about it and had always assumed she would be a mother one day. But she accepted the fact that she could not imagine Paul as a dad – one like her father and others she had known. He was an only child from a broken home, and seemed to relate to the family life stories that surrounded him like he related to everything else, with a sort of detached bewilderment.

"You know, when you begin to examine scenarios like that you can drive yourself crazy."

For a moment, she thought he had been reading her mind.

"What scenario?"

"The Seraphim Society." Poof, back on topic. "I mean, this is the only thing really linking all three of the murder victims, yet it's extremely puzzling to try to figure how that could be involved."

Their server brought their food, and they ate quietly, comparing notes on the meal. They shared an eggplant parmesan and a small scampi plate. She went to the ladies' room while he paid the check.

"Maybe the placement of the bodies has something to do not with the Seraphim Society but with family connections," Paul ventured as they were getting in her car. "I mean, membership is strictly honorary based on bloodlines."

"You think they might be related?"

"Could be. Distant cousins, maybe. I'll check into that tomorrow. Who knows? May be a busted will somewhere."

"I'll see what I can find out about the Seraphim Corporation, and the businesses that prospered because of the charity," Kate said, thinking of The Tide's very astute business writer, Susan Jeffries.

As they arrived at his place, she felt that she would have to initiate if she was going to stay, but he put his hand on her knee and said, "I've missed you, Kate."

That night they made love for the first time in three weeks. He was more amorous than she, and she didn't finish. But feeling the physical connection again made her feel whole.

6. The Suspect

It wasn't quite daylight when Paul's phone beeped. He grudgingly looked at the text.

"Kate, wake up! They've got a suspect."

She was dreaming of a courtroom drama, and the new dialogue fit right in. His friend Jason, who worked in booking, said word had spread that they were bringing in a guy based on an unsubstantiated confession.

"Holy cow!" Kate said. "Out of one dream and into another one."

She didn't have time to shower but cleaned and straightened up as best she could. At least she had on a different shirt and pair of jeans than she did on her last stop at headquarters, not even 24 hours ago.

"Sure, you don't want to come with me?"

He had already reclined back onto the bed and watched her as she put on some makeup at a mirror by the bay window.

"No, I try to stay away from the place." He nodded to the irony. "As you know."

She kissed him, then quickly repaired the damage to the lipstick she had just put on.

"You should be running the place," she said, rushing out the bedroom door.

"Thanks, babe." In his being, he knew she was right, even if it could never be.

Kate was the only reporter there when they brought the suspect in, and it was a good thing. She was going in the front door when two officers emptied the guy from a squad car in the back. She didn't get a picture, but she did see Armstrong coming into the check-in area with a clipboard in his hand.

"I can't tell you a thing," he said, waving her off with his other hand as he tried to walk by. She stepped in his path just enough that to pass would require male rudeness.

"Everything will have to wait for the lieutenant. It's way too early in the investigation..."

"For a legitimate suspect?"

He tried again to brush by. She stood her ground. He had to answer to get away.

"Not for attribution? Yes! But don't let that stop the press from lynching the guy."

That statement jarred her sufficiently for him to step around. She was right on his heels going down the corridor to his office.

"What are you talking about?" she said. "OK, not for attribution: who is the guy?"

"You know I can't tell you that. He hasn't been charged."

"Alright, in for questioning then? Where's he come from?"

He paused. "Around."

By this point, they had reached his glassed-in cubby hole and he was trying to shut the door. She was in the way.

"Around! That doesn't sound very specific."

Armstrong let out a big sigh.

"Look, Kate. I appreciate the fact that you got a boyfriend who sometimes knows what's going on sometimes before I do. I appreciate the fact that you're here, getting the news. That's your job. And you got it. You got it first: we have a person of interest, and we're questioning him. Now, I've got a report to write."

He held up the clipboard toward her face as he tried again to shut the door.

"Just tell me what you're putting in the report. I'll tell you what words I'll use, and you can tell me if they're appropriate. I know Lieutenant Long is guarded about publicity..."

"Yes, he does like to be the center of attention. Now, I'll tell you this – NOT for attribution, because all of it will have to come from him – this man is currently homeless. But he hasn't always been. He's not a bum. An alcoholic, maybe, but not a bum.

"He told an acquaintance that he had killed all three of the victims. He told us the same thing when we went to pick him up this morning at a household where he has been known to spend some weekends."

He could tell by her expression that she was already discounting this one. "It seems more plausible once you know that he was seen on surveillance video near two of the squares around the time that each of those two victims were found.

Kate thought that sounded like grounds for a thorough grilling in front of a tape recorder.

"One more thing – and this isn't just not for attribution, you can't use it at all. The suspect once worked for Mr. Pederall."

Her expression told him he had satisfied her curiosity – for the time being.

"So, I can write that police have taken in a man for questioning who was seen in the vicinity of the discovery of two of the three homicide victims whose bodies were found in city squares? And that a police source said the potential suspect, who is currently homeless, told an acquaintance that he had killed all three, but investigators have no motive?"

"Uhh, drop the last part about motive and you got it. Now, get out of here." He closed the glass door.

Kate figured she had had enough. There was no reason to hang around the police station expecting to get anything more. It would be several hours before Long arrived and could get briefed on the case, and even then, it was questionable he would even talk to her.

She decided the best thing to do was to go to the office and write up what she had, but first she wanted to get the news out that there was a suspect in custody. She jotted out the essence in a bulletin about the arrest, with a few details about the circumstances of the bodies being found. She was tempted to throw in the part about the Seraphim Society membership but reconsidered, mindful that Paul might not have had time to completely vet the information himself.

The office of The Tide was located in an artsy stretch of Bull Street which prospered by the presence of the Savannah College of Art and Design in various areas throughout the city. Its primary owner, and editor and publisher, was Ted Bridger. Ted was from Denver, by way of Atlanta, where he succeeded so well at app design and marketing that even though not yet a billionaire, he was well on his way at the young age of 38. His love of newspapers went way back to working his way through puberty by delivering the Rocky Mountain News every afternoon from 1992 to 1996.

The Tide newsroom was a large studio one flight above Dell's coffee shop and bookstore. It was about what you'd expect from a small news agency: a couple of desks with computer terminals, a comfortable couch facing a big-screen TV on the wall, a closet kitchenette and a bathroom, and a large desk by the window overlooking Bull Street for Bridger to occasionally stop by and feel kinship with the printed word. He even kept a typewriter on the desk to keep the spirit.

The reporters, a couple of dozen in all, worked mostly from home, or on the move, like Kate. They were paid by retainers to cover their field, like the crime beat, or in some cases a community, such as Tybee Island. Their job was to know what was going on – in education, municipal government, the port, and trade, or whatever – and to file digital stories about developments of interest to the general public. Bonuses were issued based on the number of hits an article, photo or video received, so there was always an in, or incentive to produce. Fewer than half the reporters had the authority to file directly to the web. Most of them seldom had the need to anyway. A couple of part-time editors came in more or less when they felt like it to edit and refresh the site, and to push the buttons for a contractor to print several hundred 16-page tabloid editions Monday, Wednesday and Friday. Bridger paid high school students to pick up the papers from the printing contractor each day and place them in news racks dotted about the city.

So far it was a financial bust for Bridger. It was an expensive, if laid-back, operation, and Ted had no idea how much it would cost him to ever turn profitable – if that was ever possible.

Meanwhile, the job suited Kate just fine. It provided just enough income, considering her own savings and not having to pay for a place to live. But mainly she liked the people and the work environment. She was reminded of that when she smelled fresh coffee from the kitchenette as she made her way up the stairway.

Robert Earl, one of the two copy editors, was plugging away at one of the computers.

"Robert Earl, you're definitely the man. I smelled that coffee a block away."

"Morning, Kate. I got in early after I saw your news alert this morning about a suspect. Figured it might be a busy day. Great work, by the way!"

"Coming from you, that's a real compliment. I appreciate it very much."

"Don't mention it."

Robert Earl Morgan would recognize good work in the news business. He had been part of a Pulitzer Prize-winning team investigating political payoffs and developers in suburban Atlanta before being lured back by his hometown paper, The Savannah Morning News. Unfortunately, he came back just as the whole print news industry hit the skids, and some of the first layoffs claimed his job under the principle of last-hired, first-fired.

She poured herself a few ounces of what could pass as black molasses on the color scale and almost an equal amount of milk into a blue-and-white SCAD mug, added a couple of spoons of raw sugar and stirred. She plopped back on the couch and held the mug with both hands on her midriff.

"I came in today because there's a whole lot of new information. I thought I could wrap up what we know at this point and the serial killing could top the front page for a while.

"Newswise, the next logical thing is the identity of the suspect, if and when he's charged."

Robert Earl laughed. "These days, that's a big if. They often seem to jump the gun, arrest the wrong person, and then have to release them."

"Better than having them release the right person," Kate said, causing Robert Earl to chuckle again.

Kate got up and moved to the other terminal desk.

"This is a good mystery. Complete with a secret society."

"What do you mean?"

"Well, maybe not so secret. But a society, anyway."

She told him about the odd link connecting the Square Murders victims, as the local media had taken to calling them. He had heard of the Seraphim Society, but not the corporation.

"You should ask Susan Jeffries about it," he said, referring to The Tide's top business correspondent, another local newspaper veteran who also worked for the Chamber of Commerce for more than a decade.

"Yeah? Is she up on this sort of thing?"

"You can ask her. She's coming in today. I don't know what time, though."

Kate got a text from Barbara: “Call me as soon as you can this morning.”

She clicked “Call” right away.

“Thank you, dear. I didn’t want to alarm you, but from a medical standpoint I didn’t realize how fast your mother has declined, since just last week. We have to get her into the hospital for evaluation.”

Kate was stunned. A dozen different thoughts and wild imaginings flashed through her head.

“Should I call an ambulance?”

“No, that won’t be necessary. It’s not critical, but I’m afraid it’s getting there fast.”

“Alright. I’ll be out as soon as I can this morning. I’m at the office now. There’s been a development in the murder case, but nothing’s happening right now.”

Kate sat in the numbness that follows a sudden, heavy dose of life outside the dream.

“I’m sorry,” Robert Earl said. “I overheard.”

She put her folded hands to her face, resting her chin on her thumbs. “Thank you.” Her long, slender fingers intertwined. “It’s all happening so fast. I guess I knew she would never get well, but I’m kind of used to things the way they were.”

A tear rolled down each cheek, and she dabbed at them with her forefinger.

“Can I get you anything?”

“No, no.” She arose from the couch and poured the rest of the coffee in the sink. Then she texted Susan to find out what time she was coming in.

The phone dinged back a moment later, but it wasn’t the business writer. Armstrong texted that Lieutenant Long was having a press briefing at 9:30. He would announce the identity of the suspect and details that led to the arrest.

7. Questions, Questions

Kate messaged Barbara to say that she wouldn't be at her mom's house until afternoon. She got back a heart emoji, which meant that was alright.

As soon as she got in the car her phone rang. It was Susan, saying she expected to be in around 11:00. She told her about the news conference.

"Well, come back to the office and update your story. We can talk then. What is it you wanted to know?"

Kate told her about the Seraphim Society connection.

"Hmm, I don't know if it's relevant or not, but there is something going on there. I'll explain later. It's nothing you could bring up at the news conference -- or would want to bring up in public."

Kate was intrigued. But as she turned into the lot across the street from headquarters, with the weight of concern about her mother, she was beginning to tire of going there. This was the third time in the past 24 hours.

"OK, ladies and gentlemen, let's get this started," Lt. Long was saying as she entered the briefing room.

Everyone was there. The Fox station had one of its network anchors, flown in the night before just in time to capture the break in Savannah's serial killing case.

"Savannah Metro police arrested this morning a Patrick Cummings, age 57, and charged him with the murder of Frederick Wallace Pederall III of Savannah, whose remains were found early yesterday in Franklin Square."

A ripple of media energy surged through the room; cameras

trained on the detective under the lights. Hands were shooting up among the couple of dozen reporters seated and standing, and some were beginning to speak.

"Mr. Cummings, who currently has no known permanent address, is also considered a person of interest in two other separate slayings last year, of Nancy Oliver and Max Long... I'll take questions in a minute ... but no one has been charged in those crimes.

"We have a witness who says Cummings admitted that he had killed all three victims, and he told officers the same thing, but we have not substantiated his claims."

"Then why is he charged?" Channel 9's Amanda Rains shot in.

"Mr. Cummings," Long said loudly, as a reminder that he had not yielded the floor to questions, "was observed through video surveillance near the scene where two of the victims were found – Mr. Pederall was one of them."

"Which was the other?" Kate asked.

"We won't say at this point while the matter is being investigated," Long said, annoyed that his prepared statement was curtailed.

"Is it true that Cummings once worked for Pederall? In what capacity?" It was Todd Worlick of the all-news radio 99.7.

"Drat," Kate thought. "He's been talking to Armstrong, too. Or somebody."

"Again, it's too early in the investigation to comment, but there is reason to believe that Mr. Cummings had prior association with that particular victim."

"Does that make him a more credible suspect?" said James Havner, the Fox News correspondent flown in for the story.

"Certainly, in crimes of this nature, the closer a perpetrator is to a victim the more likely we're able to find evidence of a motive and opportunity, two factors that may be necessary to obtain a conviction."

"So, basically, what you have at this point is a possibly bogus confession to serial killing?" Havner pressed, attempting to goad Long into revealing something else.

"We have evidence linking the suspect, Mr. Cummings, to one of the murder victims in a series of what we believe to be three targeted killings.

"Furthermore, he has confessed to the crime. All matters involved in this case are still under investigation. That's all we have at this time."

Long started folding up papers on the podium in front of him as he was peppered with questions from the gaggle of press in the room. The only one he answered was about Cummings' first court appearance.

"An arraignment is expected early this afternoon at the Chatham County Courthouse before Judge Blaine. You'll have to get details from the court."

The reporters and TV crews began filing out of the room, some gathering in small clusters to discuss the merits of the case.

"There's no way in hell this guy did this," Worlick was saying to no one in particular.

"It all follows a familiar pattern," Havner said. "As soon as they figure out they've got a serial killer on their hands they have to come up with a suspect as soon as possible. I've seen it in cases all over the country."

"You better believe it!" Worlick said. "And with Saint Patrick's Day coming up... Man, you know the city fathers want this case settled!"

Kate glanced at her phone. She had a message from Barbara.

"Your mother did eat this morning. I had to feed her, but she seemed to enjoy it. Last night before bed she wouldn't even take a bite. We do need to talk, but it can wait until later."

"I'll see you about four or five, then." Kate texted back.

She started to try to talk to Armstrong but figured he was probably already in hot water with Long for leaking some details earlier. She headed to her car on what was turning out to be a balmy morning for February.

Pigeons scattered in the sandy parking lot and some fluttered to nearby grass as she walked by.

Driving around several of the squares on her way back to the office, she wondered what possible significance they could have on the disposal of the bodies. Or the fact that different means were used to kill each victim. Obviously, the killer would have to know them, or known who they were. And he – or she – would have to have access as well as a motive, no matter how bizarre and twisted it might be.

Back on Bull Street at The Tide's office, Kate used one of the terminals to pound out details of the story so far. She left out the part about the Seraphim Society, thinking it would be confusing to the reader. Besides, apparently, she was the only reporter on it, and there was no reason to tip off anybody else at this point. Not until she could explain it, anyway.

Still, it was a pretty good yarn. This was the one that was going to stay at the top for some time to come, or so she thought. You never could tell with the Savannah press. Sometimes they got distracted by the strangest diversions.

And a lot of people in the city would just as well divert. No one wanted to cut into Saint Patrick's Day weekend and its million visitors spending a good portion of their net pay drinking green beer.

Kate glanced at the weather on her phone and also noticed it was 11:14. At that moment, Susan Jeffries walked in.

"Let me get a cup and, I'll join you on the couch. You're gonna love what I've got to tell you. It's all about cotton."

8. King Cotton

The Cotton Exchange was known as "King Cotton's Palace" when it was built on East Bay Street in the late 19th century. The title celebrated a long and prosperous history of cotton and Savannah, one which began with the development of a mechanical short-staple cotton gin by Eli Whitney at the nearby Mulberry Grove Plantation in 1793.

The device, which removes fibers attached to the seeds inside the pods, or bolls, of the cotton plant, vastly decreased the amount of time needed for a task that had been performed largely by hand. It turned upland short cotton into a profitable crop and made ports like Savannah rich. From 1830 to 1850, the number of bales produced in the United States quadrupled to almost 3 million.

Unfortunately, also quadrupling was the number of African slaves, from 700,000 in 1790 to more than 3 million in 1850. One offshoot of the cotton gin was increasing dependence on the plantation economy and slave labor, which eventually so divided the country that it led to secession of the Southern states.

After the Civil War, cotton again became vital to the economy. When the exchange was created in 1872, Georgia was the leading producer in the country with export revenue of $40 million – big bucks for a port like Savannah. But by the time the red brick exchange building on East Bay was built in 1886, the reign of the king was limited.

Cotton was selling for only 10 cents a pound when the building opened, and an unseen pest – the boll weevil – was about to destroy the crop. The tiny beetles, which infest the cotton plant, migrated from Mexico, and soon affected farmers throughout the South. Many of them were out of business by the 1920s.

"Phineas Pendleton saw it all coming," Susan Jeffries said. She was telling Kate the history of the Seraphim company and charity as they sat on the couch in The Tide's office.

"Pendleton was the chairman of the board. He, and all the directors and officers of Seraphim, came from a group of old-line Savannah families who had founded the company in the late 18th century. Most of the men – they were all men in those days, naturally – descended from one or more genealogical lines rooted in the old wards."

"In other words," Kate said, "their lineage goes back virtually to the founding of the city?"

"Correct. Now, what makes Pendleton important is that he foresaw the day that property and income taxes would be the predominant means of government revenue. Early on, he advocated converting assets to some sort of charitable foundation, which he believed correctly would be protected from such taxation.

"That's where the Seraphim Society comes in. Gradually, they converted more and more to the foundation, until finally...."

"Paul explained all that to me: How they set up new businesses individually and in groups which profited from doing business with the charity."

"Exactly! There were enormous holdings in real estate. Someone has to manage it, sell some of it when necessary, develop it in one way or another. There were commissions to be made and profits to be skimmed. In agriculture, someone has to provide the farm equipment, feedstocks, etc., the loans to keep the farms solvent during hard times.

"And that's only a sample. The biggest success story of all behind the corporation was through the export of cotton. Pendleton foresaw that the demise of that one business would be enough to bring them all down. They diversified enough, quickly enough, that they were able to get out of cotton completely by 1900, and by then the corporation itself was almost completely dissolved."

"OK, fast forward to today," Kate interjected. "What's that got to do with our serial killing, other than that the victims are all honorary members of the society?"

Susan shook her head. "Maybe it doesn't ...

"But you've heard of Lindsey Weatherford?"

Kate did a quick scan of her brain's database. "The billionaire developer?"

"Sure. He was a pioneer in coastal resorts. Well, anyway, he's the chairman of the foundation's board now. And he's set up a proposal that considerable assets of the society be returned to private use under a provision of the trust when it was established in the 1890s. It would be transferred proportionately according to the shares held by the original family corporate stockholders."

"Millions of dollars would be involved," Kate guessed.

"Billions, in fact." She allowed a moment or two for it all to sink in.

"The problem is, not all of these descendants want for this to happen."

Kate's eyes widened. "And how serious is this dispute?"

"Serious enough that lawsuits have been filed. I've got copies of two of them here." She pulled out some folded documents from her bag. Kate hurriedly scanned them.

"I see Weatherford in here, but none of the three victims."

"No, I didn't necessarily think you would. I have no idea of the extent of their involvement in the legal battle, or even if they have any. Like I told you on the phone, I know none of this is ready for the public. I just wanted you to know, in case you can find out.

"You might want to talk to Ted and decide. I don't know how much of this he would be willing to pursue."

As if on cue, Ted Bridger walked into the office and strode

straight to his desk. "Hello, ladies."

Kate asked Susan if she would stay and talk to Ted with her.

"No, I'm not that invested in this theory," she said. "Good luck with it."

As Sue picked up her bag and left, Kate walked over to Ted's desk.

"I just want to tell you what a great job you've been doing" he said. "I know it cut into your weekend, and I'm going to give you another bonus on whatever you pick up from the internet. Already your initial story has more hits globally than anything we've ever had."

"Well, good. I'm glad we're leading the story, and I want to stay on top. That's what I want to talk to you about."

She told him of the bizarre connection tying the three victims, and of the Seraphim Society, the late family held corporation, and the attempt by Weatherford to convert the holdings.

He listened with interest but seemed not to understand her point.

"Kate, we're doing really well. This story is your greatest achievement since you've been with us. You're beating everybody just covering the news. Isn't that enough? Just report the news, and let the police solve the crime?"

Suddenly, she felt deflated. The mystery had given her a thrill. She felt like part of it and imagined a role in the entire affair. Quickly, she felt diminished: She wasn't a serious investigative reporter after all; she was just Kate Cooper, knocking about the cop shops in her hometown.

"Just don't worry about it. You're doing great," Ted said as he delved into the copy she had just written and prepared to update the top of the website and send the paper to the printer.

"You've validated your idea of a police beat. As web traffic increases for breaking news, more and more tourists are exposed to The Tide and are likely to pick up a copy in their hotel or on the street. Advertisers love the increased circulation in both that and the local demographic.

"I don't think investigative work will pay off any more than that. Readers and viewers look elsewhere for that."

9. A Trolley Trio

Mainly, Kate just felt tired. She left the office and caught up with Paul's trolley tour at Monterrey Square. He was explaining to the tourists about one of Savannah's most famous crimes. Antiques dealer Jim Williams' trials for the 1981 killing of his lover in the Mercer House where he lived on Monterrey Square was the basis for John Berendt's book *Midnight in the Garden of Good and Evil,* which had attracted an interest in Savannah that reached globally.

Frank Miller was on the trolley, with Howell Barker. Sometimes they met up with Paul this way. Like Howell, Frank was a local history enthusiast who had once driven the same tour route as Paul. He seemed to be listening intently to the type of spiel that he must have delivered himself hundreds of times, as if grading her boyfriend on his performance.

If Kate could describe Frank in one word, it would be "sallow." He looked like the old timers who were still around on her first newspaper job, guys who had worked in newsrooms for 40 years and smoked a million cigarettes in that time.

In fact, Miller had been a reporter in his youth. Most of his career he was a history teacher, though, before retiring and conducting tours. And although he once smoked tobacco he no longer did.

Frank was no more sociable than Howell. He seemed thrown off when Kate sat next to him, as if maybe he didn't recognize her at first.

"Hello, Frank."

"Oh, hi Kate," he said, as she slipped into the seat.

"What's new?" she asked.

Chat like that didn't resonate with Frank.

"I guess in this business it's more of a matter of what's old?"

That also fell flat. She didn't press any further conversation as they listened to Paul tell a couple dozen other trolley riders about how Jim Williams was the only person in Georgia ever to stand trial four times for the same crime. The final time, after two overturned convictions and one mistrial, Williams was acquitted of murder in the death of Danny Hansford, but he died unexpectedly the following year.

"The house today," Paul closed, "is called the Mercer-Williams House, honoring both Williams, who was a noted historic preservationist here in Savannah, and the original owner, General Hugh Weedon Mercer, the great-grandfather of songwriter Johnny Mercer."

As Paul steered the trolley around the corner toward the next and final stop before heading back to the Visitors Center, Howell leaned over from his seat in the back and said, "Well, Kate, it looks like murder is just part of Savannah tradition."

"Even so, I'd say the latest ones are a little different," Kate said.

"By an order of magnitude," added Frank, who seemed to be coming out of a mental slumber. "But what's the difference? Jim Williams was right. He saw Savannah society for what it is."

"What is that Frank?" Kate asked.

"Hypocrites and liars. Mostly slugs," he said like a biologist describing a species.

"The very idea of basing any kind of hierarchy on family name is ridiculous. It doesn't take too many generations to thoroughly dilute whatever qualities that might have made an ancestor a success. Why, at just the level of your great grandparents the man who provides your name supplies just one-eighth your DNA."

"Cool! Then I represent at least five continents," Kate said.

That elicited a laugh from both Frank and Howell. She was pleased to have amused Paul's friends.

They were rolling up to Chatham Square, named for the British prime minister William Pitt, Earl of Chatham, who in the 18th century before the American Revolution was an advocate for the rights of American colonists. Chatham County, surrounding Savannah, also bears his name.

"This Mediterranean Revival home, built in 1906," Paul was saying, "is the former home of the Barnard Street School. The almost 21,000-foot structure with tapered bell tower was renovated in 2009 by the Savannah College of Art and Design and today is named Pepe Hall."

Kate was stuck on Howell's remark about the current murders making history.

"Listen, one of these days historic tours of Savannah will include the story of our murders at every square where a body is found."

Howell seemed to consider that a likely possibility, and the way Frank was gleaming Kate could tell that he did, too.

Soon they were pulling up to the Visitors Center to drop off the passengers. Howell and Frank also got off.

"Kate, we were going to grab some lunch. You want to join us," Paul said. "We're going to be discussing a topic close to your heart."

She let out an exaggerated gasp. "I don't think I could take any more of it. Besides, I am absolutely exhausted. I'm just going over to your place and crash for a couple of hours before going back out to Mom's."

"OK, I'll fill you in if we come up with anything."

He gave her a slight peck on the lips and squeezed her hand. She got out her phone and ordered up an Uber.

10. Family Lines

It took a while for Kate to drift off. She couldn't get the story out of her mind. Finally, when she did, she had restless dreams about being a little girl and being chased through the park by some strange force that she couldn't see but felt compelled to either hide from or flee.

When she awoke, Paul was sitting in his big recliner in the other room, clicking away on his laptop. She stood at the doorway between the two rooms, glancing at his back. He turned suddenly.

"Oh, hey, babe. Research is turning up some pretty good stuff."

It took a moment or two for her head to clear enough to recall what he was referring to. "What have you found?"

"Well, for starters, these families go back farther than you'd think." She stepped over and placed her hand gently on his shoulder.

"Records from the colony's trustees reveal the names and occupations and status of the colonists, and their obligations to the colony to pay for their passage and whatever land they received.

"Those who paid their own passage also often bought their own land. Either way it was not the paradise that anyone might have imagined.

"A considerable number were marked as 'fled the colony' or 'run away to Carolina.'

"Some returned to England. One of them was recorded as fleeing Georgia and returning with the Reverend John Wesley."

"I know I told you earlier about how life revolved around the wards in the early days. Bloodlines spread as they would anywhere, with children moving on and intermarrying. But some of these folks were so exclusive that they basically remained within the same ward for generations – sometimes for a century or more.

“And it was families like that who founded the Seraphim Corporation and held it together.”

He stood and pointed to the computer screen, which was next to some sort of chart or diagram he had drawn on what looked like the carboard sheet that comes with folded dry-cleaned shirts.

“Look at this. Here are the family trees of our three murder victims, and here is a map of the locations where their bodies were found.

Kate stared at what seemed to be an impossible maze of names and staggered lines. Next to it was a historic map of the downtown, with various symbols and circles drawn across some of the squares.

“What are these lines here?”

Paul quickly turned his head to her, eager to share his revelation.

“That's just it! This shows clearly how the lineage of each murder victim can be traced through at least one line of ancestry all the way back.”

Kate didn't quite get it.

“All the way back to what?”

“All the way back to the ward surrounding the square where their body was found!”

“You're so smart to figure all this out,” Kate said. “How come you can't figure out how to fix your motorcycle?”

“That, my dear, takes more than brains. It takes skill, and I don't have the dexterity, or one-eighth the DNA, as Frank would say to handle a monkey wrench.”

11. Method or Madness

Kate felt a renewed vigor on her way to see her mother. The work Paul had done put these killings in a whole new light. This was not the work of some homeless guy. And probably not even a psychopathic killer. There had to be a method behind it, but it looked far more likely that the method involved some sinister dealings involving big money rather than the derangement of one individual.

Possibly, the killer – or killers – had chosen this means of disposal of the victims to throw off investigators. Make it look like the work of a madman, with an underlying logic that would never be unravelled.

Her mother was in bed when Kate arrived at about 4 p.m., but she was awake and smiled at the sight of her daughter. Barbara occupied the rocker by the window.

"She ate breakfast and sat in the den for a little while this morning. By noon she was ready to sleep some more."

"Well done!" Her mother beamed even more as Kate stepped over and gave her a hug.

"Hang on for a minute. I'll come get you and we'll get something more to eat. Maybe go out!"

Barbara had already stepped down the hallway to the den. Kate joined her.

"So, what do you think?"

Barbara twisted her head to the side and sighed. "She does seem to be getting better. But I don't want to be the one to say for sure."

Kate felt an immediate letdown after seeing her mom look so well for a change.

"It's just that, at this stage of stroke recovery things can go either way," Barbara continued, "In the hospital, they have the instruments to measure her physical condition."

Kate thought for a moment, her hands folded at her chin.

"When?"

"Now would be as good a time as any."

"To the emergency room?"

"I've already called ahead. Just in case you'd want to go this evening. I spoke with a friend on night duty at Candler. She told me to take her to a clinic in the back of the hospital that is set up to handle just this sort of admission."

"Good to know." Kate reached out and hugged her friend. "What would I do without you?"

Barbara stifled a laugh. "Why, I know you'd carry on no matter what, Kate Cooper. I'm just glad I'm here to help."

Together they cleaned, changed, and dressed Katherine, got her in the car, and Kate drove her to Candler Hospital. Right away, she discovered that despite her instructions for the brain clinic, she still had to register her mother first at the emergency room.

That meant getting a wheelchair, rolling her mom back through the maze of the hospital complex, and then wheeling her back.

While she was in the ER, she heard the man in line in front of her say his name was Herbert Pederall. He went over and sat in a chair in the corner behind the entrance as she got the paperwork for her mom.

Leaving the wheelchair in its spot near the registration desk, she walked over to the man, who was short, well-dressed, and appeared to be in his mid-50s.

"Excuse me, but are you related to Frederick Wallace Pederall?"

His eyes widened behind his glasses, making them appear even larger. He looked both ways and then straight at her, his face registering intense alarm.

"Who are you?"

"I'm Kate Cooper, and..."

"I don't care, I'm not signing," he said, quickly standing and looking hurriedly this way and that, as if seeking the exit. "You people... you have some nerve. Why can't you leave me alone?"

"But I'm with The Tide," she said as he brushed past her and rushed out the glass door to the outside. "The newspaper..."

It was too late. He was already out on the sidewalk, looking around as if he was very agitated.

"Wonder what that was all about?" Kate said to herself. She knew now it was best she go on about her own affairs and let him take care of whatever medical need he might have. An ER nurse arrived at her side that moment, and with him she started rolling her mom's wheelchair down the corridor back toward the brain clinic.

After getting her mother admitted, and going with her to her room where she was hooked up to an IV and monitors to gauge the function of her heart and brain, Kate couldn't stand the thought of going back to the house.

She texted Paul and told him she would be going back to his place, gave him a rundown of the trip to the hospital and told him she would fill him in later. He messaged back that he had some things to take care of, including going to see his dad, who lived in a nursing home on Skidaway Road.

The behavior of Herbert Pederall in the ER was so mysterious that Kate felt she had to get to the bottom of it despite Ted's advice not to try to solve the crime but to merely report it. She dropped by the office and was relieved to see that Ted was not there, or anyone else for that matter.

She scanned through old city directories, phone books and whatever else she could find to see if she could come up with others who had connections to the Seraphim Foundation. In addition to Herbert Pederall, she found five who lived in the Savannah area. Two of them were named Greene, a Richard on Hilton Head Island and Sarah in town. There was another Nancy Oliver, besides the one who became the second murder victim, and a Christopher Long, possibly related to Max Long, victim No. 2.

The fifth prospect was a Jeremy Swift. He lived in Pooler, she could tell from an address on his Facebook account, but she couldn't turn up a phone number anywhere. Since Richard Greene lived on Hilton Head, in South Carolina, Kate devised a plan to call him for an appointment, heading east on I-16 to try to find Swift and then north on I-95 to the Hilton Head exit.

"Well, I'd be glad to talk to you, but I don't know much about it," he said. "I don't keep up much with it. Get a newsletter now and then."

"Well, if you can just tell me what you know. Every little bit helps, and there are so few of you around who are as close to the situation."

"Really? I'd never thought of it that way, but I guess you're right. I can't see you until after four. I'm going to play tennis after a while."

"Very well. I'll call when I'm on my way."

"Can't we just do this on the phone?"

"I'm sorry, but some of the information might be sensitive to discuss over the phone. It's best that I see you in person." Kate felt sure that he could get her meaning and would be prepared for her type of questions when she got there.

"OK. I don't know what you might mean, but as I said, I'll be glad to help. You seem like a nice young lady."

"Thank you, sir. I'll be there before five, for sure."

Kate was relieved to find she was getting out of downtown and onto the highway before rush hour. Traffic could be slow on I-16. Pooler was a booming bedroom community quickly becoming a commercial hub as well for thousands of people who lived west of town and out near the Savannah-Hilton Head airport.

The address she had for Jeremy Swift turned out to be a complex of townhomes for retirees and the semi-retired. A man who appeared to be in his mid-60s was watering a small patch of grass in front with a garden hose.

Kate rolled down her window. "Are you Jeremy Swift."

He gave her a cautious stare. "I'm Jerry Swift. What can I do for you?"

She got out, told him who she was and what she was doing, and he invited her inside. They sat in a small parlor in the front, on what looked like antique chairs. He explained that he was a retired accountant and a widower and had moved from downtown two years earlier to be closer to his daughter and grandchildren.

After a few preliminary questions, in which Kate revealed a sketch of the theory concerning serial murders and the foundation, Swift seemed to be either confused or circumspect.

"What is it that you're saying? That you think Lindsey Weatherford is trying to intimidate people? And that some are being killed because of this?" He seemed very concerned, fearful even.

That threw Kate off. She felt like she was giving out more than she was taking in.

"No, no. You see..."

"This is ghastly!" He looked now as if he was about to turn ill. "I can only say that this sounds like that bunch. Good Lord, I wonder who is next."

Kate thought it best to tamp down the speculation that she had just started.

"Look, I came to you to see if you knew anything about this. I'm sorry if I upset you. There's certainly nothing so far to substantiate my theory."

At this, he seemed to lighten up a bit.

"Oh, I don't think there's any reason to come after me. Like I say, I don't keep up with it. I got solicitations and offers in the mail, but I just threw them away. I don't care what they do with the foundation. My proxy belongs to Weatherford's wife, June, anyway. She's my cousin, and I've never seen any reason not to let her handle things for our family's side. Now, I'm not so sure."

"Well, once again, I'm sorry I bothered you," Kate said, getting up. "I don't even know if I'll continue with this idea. I feel sure if there was anything to it you would know something."

"Well, you should continue. How's anybody going to find out if people like you don't look into it." He saw her back to the door, and soon she was heading up I-95 toward Hilton Head.

Jerry Smith may have been a bust when it came to getting new information, but he certainly seemed on edge – like Herbert Pederall at the hospital. And he seemed to have little doubt that the characters in play may be capable of murder. The question is: Did he know that or just have some inclination to think the worst of people with power.

U.S. 278 out to Hilton Head was jammed with vehicles, all heading at a breakneck pace through the jungle of development that had occurred over the past 45 years as the island resort had mushroomed. Bluffton was South Carolina's fastest growing city for several years running, and the roadways around and through it resembled Atlanta more than it did the relaxed, quasi-natural environment across the bridge.

Richard Greene lived in Palmetto Dunes, one of the earliest of the vacation and retiree home developments. Kate was ushered in by a Hispanic maid to a shady brick patio where Greene sat by a white, wrought-iron table bearing a pitcher of iced tea.

After a few pleasantries, Kate decided to skip the feelers and come straight to the point. She quickly outlined everything she had learned and observed, including the alarm that Swift seemed to experience. When she was done, there was a moment of silence. Then, Greene broke into a roaring laugh.

"You can't be serious," he said. "Oh, my God, you are!"

Kate was embarrassed but not enough to backtrack.

"Murder is a serious matter."

Greene nodded in agreement. "Yes, but this..." He took a sip of tea and looked at her earnestly.

"My dear young lady..." His look had turned into one of pity almost. "Someone must have been playing a prank."

Her expression remained the same: blank curiosity. He understood that she wasn't joking.

"In all honesty," he said, "I can assure you that nothing like your theory is involved with these killings. Why, for one thing, Lindsey Weatherford has everything he needs locked up. Why would he do such a thing?

"I know, there are always a few malcontents, a few resisters to any proposal. About anything, really. But I think you'll find that the people at the top of this organization know both what they're doing and how to get it accomplished – well short of killing people. A century or so ago, maybe, but not these days."

Kate left feeling discouraged but not defeated. It was a good hour back to Savannah this time of day, and she still had three foundation members to go.

Sarah Greene and Christopher Long flat-out refused to talk to her. It was hard to tell if either of them were fearful or just annoyed. With Nancy Oliver, it was a different matter.

"The late Nancy was my namesake and my cousin, on my mother's side. She was a Janston," the woman told Kate, after reluctantly letting her inside her small but well-appointed apartment in a row of houses near Warren Square.

"We always considered her like an aunt because she was 20 years older. The Janstons and the Olivers are both old-time Savannah families, and Nancy became the one in that branch who handled all the affairs of the foundation."

She shuddered slightly. "I know she was concerned about Weatherford's plans, even if no one else was. She made her concerns known, too. My aunt – cousin, actually – was never a shrinking violet behind the scenes of a controversy.

"Would she take her opposition so far as to risk her life? Or would the principals involved go so far as to try to eliminate her? I don't know if that's even possible. She certainly would not have thought so.

"But I can tell you this: These three deaths certainly have people talking, especially those who know about Aunt Nancy's stubborn determination. Now, I don't know about the other two."

"Did you know Max Long?"

"Like someone you'd see every year or so, at a reunion or a board meeting of some kind. We're related by family vaguely."

"Is Christopher Long related?"

"Christopher? I think Chris is a grandson. The father's dead, I believe."

She paused as Kate jotted down a couple of notes on her phone.

"You're sure you wouldn't use my name?"

"No, I'm just making a couple of notations, just to keep track. This is very complex." The woman nodded. "Do you know how the process of returning assets from the Foundation works?" Kate asked.

"No, I don't. Listen, you'll have to excuse me. I really can't tell you anything more than what I've said." She arose, and as Kate fumbled with her phone and bag she added: "It is complex, and hard to understand. Given to rational light, I'm sure it could have nothing to do with these murders."

"Given to rational light." Those words rang in Kate's ears as she made her way back toward her car. Nothing seemed rational about the whole affair.

12. Warnings

Kate felt like she was trying to get inside her own head. There was too much going on all at once – her mother's rapid decline, being at the epicenter of a major murder mystery, a strange homesickness for D.C., and most of all her relationship with Paul.

She thought about him all the time, and imagined conversations with him when he was not around. More importantly, she genuinely liked being with him, just being in the presence of his company. And even if she didn't, she was bound by the strongest physical attraction imaginable.

At the same time, he remained so aloof in so many ways. When they were with others, she felt like just one of the gang, And the absence of affection in public was so striking that in a crowd one was more likely to guess that they were sister and brother. Kate didn't know what to do about that; much less, his seeming indifference to the future.

Politically, he was more conservative than Kate, which she attributed to time spent in the military and law enforcement. She accused him of dreaming of a paramilitary state run by robots, and he argued that it would be more just in the end.

Right now, she didn't know what to do but to get back to practical realities at hand. It looked like she had some time on her hands, so she headed to Gilroy's Pub, a watering spot popular with politicians, police, and news hounds. It was a pleasant evening, so she sat outside in the garden. She ordered a margarita and was just being served when Armstrong walked by on Liberty Street and spotted her. He walked around to the entrance, and as she was sipping the first edge of salt off the rim, he pulled up a chair.

"Well Kate, have you solved our case yet?"

"No, I'm waiting on you guys to do that. Since you reminded me of my proper place as a journalist, that is."

"Good. I'm glad you paid attention." He signaled the barman to send over a draft. "Anything new?"

She told him the Seraphim angle and about her conversations with the heirs.

"Whoa, you've been busy. We won't have to worry about you getting in our way very long, because when word gets around of what you're digging into you're going to be gone."

"What do you mean?"

Armstrong leaned across the table as if what he was about to say was highly confidential.

"If you think a man like Lindsey Weatherford is going to let a reporter go around making insinuations that he's a serial killer... without any proof, or even any real evidence..."

"I'm not saying he's a serial killer!"

"What, then?"

Kate thought for a moment. "Maybe he sent out orders to get some people in line. And maybe whoever he sent to do it got carried away..."

"Ha! In fact, ha, ha!" He took a long pull on the frosty mug that had just arrived, laughing through his eyes. His condescension cut to her spine.

"What, then? Who do you think is responsible for this? Serial killers don't normally target victims based on vectors like this."

"Vectors? Oh my God, you've been talking to Paul. I knew it." He was raising his voice and immediately realized it. Lowering his tone, "I told you, Kate, leave..."

"I know, I know! Leave the investigating to the investigators. You've told me that at least a dozen times. And I didn't get this from Paul, Buster. Just a bit of luck and some hard work today tracking these people down."

"Well, for all the good it'll do you. That boyfriend of yours is just as likely a suspect as a conspiracy involving Lindsey Weatherford."

Kate was usually likely to let a wisecrack pass, but there was something about this one that had an unpleasant ring to it, like a school bell to a kid starting Monday morning.

"You're not serious." The detective started taking a big gulp from his beer, but she could see his eyes averting her glare. "You are serious! What, are you insane?"

Now it was her voice that was being raised. Heads turned at other tables in the garden and inside the bar. She started getting up to go but he grabbed her arm. Not too much, just enough to get her to sit back down.

"Listen, Kate," he said, lowering his voice. "You can't use any of this, not even on background, but of course we've considered connections to the Seraphim Society. We're investigating a murder case. All our evidence so far points to a psychopathic killer who for some reason has established this pattern. An individual pattern that somehow fits into a diseased mind. That's how it works."

"But Paul...?"

He raised a hand in his defense. "I didn't say it was Paul."

She was shaking her head in disbelief. He let the moment pass.

"You're telling me that that none of this bull crap you picked up today came from your boyfriend?"

"Well..." She wasn't sure how much she should say.

"Look, who's coming up with some kind of theory involving a historical angle? Who's providing you with clues in that direction? Any killer would be pleased to have the public believe that his work was done by someone else."

He took her arm again, this time gently. She sensed arousal, something she'd been used to causing since she was 12. She jerked back.

"Kate, I'm not saying the guy's the killer, but he's no good. He's a psycho, too, believe me. Even if he wasn't, he's not good enough for you."

He reached toward her hand again, and she quickly pulled it away. She felt like turning the table over on top of him and storming out, and would have, too, if she didn't ruefully feel that she might need information from him in the future.

"Armstrong, you're completely nuts, you know that? You insult my intelligence and my capabilities as a journalist, then you tell me my boyfriend could be a psycho killer – which is to say that I don't have the good sense to avoid getting involved with a psycho killer – and then you hit on me? Unbelievable!"

He looked totally chastised.

"Kate, I'm sorry." He appeared to be groping for a way to explain his behavior.

"And wait a minute! Aren't you married?"

She was rolling her eyes and getting up once more to leave. He stopped her again.

"My wife and I... we're not getting along."

Kate put both hands on the table and looked him straight in the eye.

"Armstrong, if I slept with every guy who told me he wasn't getting any from his wife I might as well go into business."

His phone buzzed, stopping her from telling him off one last time. He looked down and his eyes popped.

"Uh, oh. We've got another body found downtown. In Orleans Square."

13. Variation on a Theme

Nothing fit about this new murder. First of all, the victim was black, middle-aged and with no family connections in a city he was visiting on business. Also, the body was found earlier in the night than the trio of white, pedigreed retirees. And it was in one of the most visible of city squares, although the police admitted it was pretty quiet and isolated at the time of the disposal of the corpse.

"It's either a crude copycat, or the killer is trying to throw everybody off," Paul told Kate as she huddled with a few other reporters under a portico at the Civic Center, across the street from Orleans Square. They were all glued to their phones, largely to keep up with what the others were reporting.

"That's what I thought. And so does probably everyone here, but the cops aren't saying anything."

"They just want the whole thing to go away," he said. "From the standpoint of the people they work for, it doesn't matter. Headlines containing the words 'serial killer' and 'Savannah' with St. Patrick's Day around the corner don't depend on reason to keep people away."

St. Pat's is the biggest time of the year for Savannah from the tourism standpoint. Hundreds of thousands of visitors descend on the city for the mid-March festival honoring the saint and the Irish heritage of a good chunk of the population. With one of the largest St. Patrick's parades anywhere, the streets are open to often boisterous revelry. Green-clad leprechauns and cloverleafs are everywhere. The city's fountains are dyed green, even the one at Orleans Square built in honor of German immigrants to Georgia.

Waves of Irish and German Catholics came to Savannah in the mid-1900s, adding to a diversity that began with Oglethorpe's settlement more than a century earlier. Still, the first Irish in the colony were Protestants, and among the earliest settlers were the Lutheran Salzburgers, who founded the Ebenezer community.

Catholicism was initially banned from Georgia. It did not gain acceptance until the American Revolution. Thousands of French, Haitian and Irish soldiers helped try to retake Savannah from the British in 1779, and Polish General Casimir Pulaski was mortally wounded in the effort. Sacrifice like that did not go unnoticed by a grateful newly independent Georgia, and religious toleration was expanded, although Catholics did not obtain full rights until adoption of the U.S. Constitution in 1789.

Orleans Square was created in 1850 in recognition of the Battle of New Orleans against the British in the War of 1812. It is one of two squares honoring the heroes of that war, the other being Chippewa Square just to the east, named for the Battle of Chippewa along the Canadian border.

Orleans Square came close to being swallowed up by development, which happened to four other Savannah squares, two of which have been restored. Just to the west of the square is the Savannah Civic Center, where Kate huddled with her colleagues as a light rainfall began. It was fast approaching 11 p.m., and the TV crews were set up for their live shots and growing impatient.

"Is anybody going to talk to us?" wailed Jan Thomas of WTOC.

As if on cue, Martha Orlando, the police public relations official, came walking out of the park square toward the Civic Center. She held a clipboard in one hand and a small megaphone in the other.

"There will be no further statement tonight. The mayor will hold a news conference tomorrow morning at 9:30 a.m., across the street in Orleans Square, where the body was found."

Collective groans went out, and Orlando was immediately bombarded with questions, which frustrated her more with each blast.

"What about the I.D. of the victim?"

Withheld until notification of relatives out of state.

"What kind of business was he here on?"

Same answer.

"Is this killing related to the other three?"

No comment. Under investigation.

"What about Patrick Cummings, the suspect being held in the Pederall death?"

"I'll have to check on that for you," Orlando said. "But I believe Mr. Cummings is still being held in connection with that slaying."

That was enough for the television reporters, who had run out of time. All of them broke out of the pack and darted over to their trucks to produce the soundbites that would make up the late-night news. Todd Worlick was the only one still asking questions, trailing Orlando on her trek back to the square like a hound dog pup looking for another treat.

Kate was just glad to get out of there and over to Paul's apartment. He wouldn't be home for another hour or so, but he'd left her a key, hooked under the pewter fish head that decorated the end of the downspout at the corner of his building.

When she got inside, she quickly updated her story and filed it on The Tide's online site. Then she remembered it was trash night, and so she took the plastic bag from the garbage can under the kitchen sink to carry back downstairs and place it in the receptacle outside. Paul only did this every week or so, she surmised. The trash was really beginning to stink.

Seeing that there were no more bags in the box under the sink, when she got downstairs, she emptied the contents of the one she had into the garbage bin in the alley, in order to reuse the one.

There, on the surface of the mound of trash in the bin, were several sheets of paper with what looked like lines of a family tree.

Closer inspection showed them to be the ancestries of the first three murder victims – Oliver, Long and Pederall.

"Not that strange," Kate thought. She knew he had been doing such research on the victims. But there was a disturbing element. The papers also had notations of some sort – like "walks in the park on Sunday evening," or "takes dog to groomers on Abercorn."

For an instant, Armstrong's words came piercing back – how Paul was a loner type, knew the history to create a pattern, had a criminal record. What if this research preceded the killings…?

Just as quickly, the nonsense of such a thing smothered out the notion. But it was too late. A moment of doubt had entered her mind. It wasn't enough that it didn't remain there. It wasn't just a question of some action that Paul had taken or his ideas. This was an admission to herself that deep inside she was capable of questioning the character of anyone – even Paul, and even if only for a moment. That thought disturbed her.

It was reassuring when Paul got home. Kate had already crawled into bed, and when he slipped in beside her, she immediately reached out and grabbed his hand. He pulled her closer and kissed her, and they made love with a passion and a tenderness she had never known.

14. Internal Strife

As daylight penetrated through the cracks in the blinds, Kate arose and checked for news alerts. Nothing. She put on coffee. Feeling very wifey for a change, she put a pat of butter in a skillet and cracked four eggs into a bowl to make an omelet. Then she buttered some wheat bread for the toaster oven.

She was pouring orange juice when she heard the toilet flush and turned around just as he walked into the room. They both broke into knowing smiles.

"What are you grinning about?" he said as he reached for a coffee mug by the sink.

She didn't say anything but popped him on the bottom as he passed.

"Calm down, Frisky," he said, pouring a cup of brew.

"I'm feeling more domestic than frisky right now," she said, whipping the eggs toward a froth.

"What time is the news conference?"

"9:30, I think. I'll have to double check."

He plopped into his recliner and began scrolling Instagram. She stirred a dash of cream into the eggs and dumped them into the hot skillet. It seemed a perfect time to ruin a perfect day. She told him about finding the research documents in the trash and the flash of doubt and fear it put in her.

"I don't know how you could get an idea like that!"

"It wasn't an idea, exactly. It was more of just a sudden feeling, a gut reaction to new information flooding in faster than the mind can process it. Must have been something Armstrong said – when

I was outlining the case for serial killings being due to something involving dissolution of the Seraphim Society.

"He threw cold water on it and said it was a psycho. No telling what he thinks now, after the fourth one."

Paul had developed a frown approaching a snarl. "So, Armstrong said it was a psycho killer and the psycho killer might be me?"

"Well... no." She could tell he was miffed. "He was just trying to say that jumping to conclusions about a man like Lindsey Weatherford would be no different to jumping to conclusions about anyone else."

"And then he gave you some reasons that someone would conclude it was me?" He was getting angry, she knew, but wasn't raising his voice. "What did you say to all of this?"

"I got up to leave! I told him off and was walking out when he got a message about the Orleans Square body." It riled her that he would doubt she would defend him, and then she felt defensive all of a sudden.

"Wait a minute, walking out of where?"

"Well, we were having drinks at Gilroy's..."

"You were having drinks with Armstrong?" This time his voice did rise to an unacceptable level. Kate was stunned.

"Not having drinks, exactly. I was having a margarita and he came in and sat down and we started talking. Don't tell me you're jealous."

He laughed. "Jealous? Of Armstrong? No, I don't like the guy, that's all, and he's stupid. I detest the guy, and you seem to feel it's alright to cozy up to him to get information for a story."

"Cozy up...?" He still wasn't listening. "Look, I can't help it if the guy comes on to me..."

"He came on to you?" This was practically a shout.

“And I left!” she said firmly. “I was walking out.”

“Alright. Never mind.” He turned to the bedroom. “We’re having a meeting down at the trolley barn. I won’t have time for breakfast.”

Kate stood there fuming, a spatula in hand. She wanted to ask something like “And when did you find out about this meeting?” but instantly was mindful that nobody told her to start breakfast.

She could see his point — if things had happened the way he put it. But it was so unfair that he jumped to conclusions about the circumstances of her meeting with Armstrong. And now he wasn’t going to listen to any more about it. Her explanation would have to just lie there, an unspoken reality of hers alone.

She found that to be frustrating to the point of maddening. The most disturbing thing about it was she couldn’t help believing that this type of misunderstanding was bound to reoccur. And this on the first day after the most exhilarating, passionate night of her life – one that had sealed a bond between her and Paul that only a few minutes earlier she thought would last forever.

Kate tossed up the omelet and had just put the bread in the oven when Paul walked back through on the way to the door. He kissed her behind the ear.

“Look, I’m sorry. I didn’t mean to question you. It just took me by surprise is all – the way it came out. I know you’re not about to two-time me with anyone, much less Armstrong.”

She smiled slightly. “And I know you’re not a serial killer.”

He turned going out the door and motioned with his raised thumb and forefinger like a pistol. “Of that, you can never be sure.”

Then added on the way out: “Incidentally, those notes you were so concerned about came from Howell. I think they were Frank’s. Something about putting themselves in the mind of a killer.”

Kate ate a few bites of the eggs and a piece of toast, glumly trying to understand what had just happened. Specious doubt had inconveniently turned into a row.

She had put on some fresh clothes, which she kept there, and was tidying up the breakfast spoils when she heard her phone buzz on the windowsill. It was Ted Bridger.

"Kate, call me when you're up," he texted.

Figuring he wanted to touch base prior to the news conference, she called right away.

"What's up, Ted?"

"Kate, this is awkward, but I don't know any other way to put this: Did you begin your own investigation into the serial killings in the name of The Tide after I told you not to?"

Kate was trying to put everything in context. True, he had told her something along the lines of "report the crime but let the investigators investigate."

"But this was more of a 'Let's find out if there is enough information out there to warrant an investigation."

Ted sighed. "Well, you've certainly gotten the attention of the folks you would investigate."

"What do you mean?"

There was a short pause. "Lindsey Weatherford called me at home this morning. Said he had heard that one of my reporters was going around asking questions about him and the Seraphim Society, implying that there may be some sort of wrongdoing, even that business related to the foundation might be involved in murder."

Kate realized that Ted was taking this by no means lightly.

"I... I don't know what to say. As I say, things started happening so fast. Bits and pieces started falling together...

"Your instincts may be good, Kate, and your sources of information are broad. It's not that I don't believe your theory, but you should have run it past me again. I had already told you no."

"I'm sorry..."

"I'm sorry, too. I'm taking you off the story, Kate."

That cut her sharply.

"What?"

He paused again. "There's no reason for you to go to the news conference this morning. The Tide will cover what the others are reporting for the time being."

"But..."

"I'm running a business here, Kate. As much fun as it is, I'm running a business. And Lindsey Weatherford is a rich and powerful man around here. If we're going to look into his dealings it has to be more discreet.

"Now, this new killing really throws a wrench in the works. We have to wait for things to settle down. Meanwhile, I'm taking action based on insubordination. The others who work here have to see that I am still the boss, as much as I like being their friend. I'm also suspending you for the time being."

"Suspending me?" She hoped he could tell from her voice how ludicrous she thought the whole thing was. Here she was, a veteran reporter from Washington, D.C., working for peanuts to keep his newspaper dream alive.

"Yes, suspending you until further notice. If you plan on doing any more investigating, you will not do it in my name."

Kate just stood in stunned silence.

"Frankly, I think you've been working too hard. And you're under a lot of pressure. The others have told me about the recent turn with your mother. Just take some time off and call me in a week. We will see how this thing goes."

She said nothing.

"Kate? Are you alright?"

She recovered enough to say, "Yeah, Ted. I'm fine. I'll call you in a week or so."

Another few seconds elapsed.

"I hope so, Kate. You're a good journalist, and I'm lucky to have you. I hope our relationship continues for a long time, but I have a feeling it won't."

As she left Paul's apartment, she felt a mood of depression falling in. First a misunderstanding with Paul, and now this: suspension for asking questions – exactly what she is supposed to do. A guy like Lindsey Weatherford shuts things down with a phone call. That's the way it always worked.

And her argument with Paul had left a bad taste. Never had she felt so much a part of him, and yet so far apart.

She headed down Abercorn in the direction of Candler Hospital. At least her recent suspension status would allow some time to do something really useful – take better care of her mom.

15. New Information

With the serial murder case seemingly behind her – though in her heart she knew she wasn't finished with it – Kate's relationship with Paul was another matter. When things from the outside upset it, even the slightest bit, he seemed to withdraw back into whatever protective mindset accommodated him.

This was one of those times when he "worked on his bike." It was just a matter of focusing on something else to take his mind off whatever troubled him at a given time.

She knew how he thought. Unless she reached out to him, he would conclude that she didn't want to talk to him – because of the argument, or a life decision, or whatever. Therefore, he would not call, or even text her. She figured if enough time elapsed, he would just write off their love as though it never existed. Well, maybe not, but she could never be sure. It baffled and frustrated her that he seemed to be able to detach himself so easily.

Growing up, she had always imagined that she one day would be married and have children. As a maturing adult, she had grown to believe that she would not. Now, she was involved with someone she had never felt about this way before. She knew she didn't want to be with anyone else.

The other side of her brain was thinking she was sitting on top of a fascinating story, and she was dying to get it out. And she wanted to be first. Truth was paramount, but she had to admit there was a thrill to the sprint and the goal. That was a reporter's instinct. She just hoped that this latest snag – practically getting fired from her job – wouldn't slow her down too much.

In a way, she wanted to break this story wide open, build up her creds and head back to Washington. Maybe take her mother with her. If Paul wanted to follow, that would have to be his decision.

At the hospital, Kate's mood lightened when Katherine smiled at her. It was not a large smile, just a crook of a grin in one corner of the mouth. But it was the intent that counted. There was a tiny sparkle in one eye, at least. It was clearly a sign of recognition, or Kate was satisfied to think so.

She waited about an hour in her mother's room before the doctor arrived. Nurses came in twice performing their morning tasks with each patient in what amounted to a four-person suite. One space was vacant, and there was a TV in the common area softly pacing through one of the morning magazine shows. The local station broke in with news from the just-ended official briefing on the body in Orleans Square.

The mayor was center stage, pattering about St. Patrick's Day and the safety of the city and how visitors should rest assured that they would not become victims of a serial killer on the loose. He added some double-talk about the beauty of Savannah this time of year and the good fortune of residents and guests alike — presumably, those who hadn't been murdered – before turning over the spotlight to the police commissioner, Jack Donnor, for details on the latest crime.

The victim's name was Robert Jackson, from Philadelphia. He was 49 years old and had been in Savannah for two weeks, staying at the Days Inn. Jackson was a troubleshooter for a company that sold various heavy equipment used along the docks. He was wrapping up a contract with the Georgia Ports Authority, where people who worked with him said he was eager to get back to his wife and two children.

Like another of the recent murder victims, his brain had been penetrated from back of the head with something like an ice pick. Evidence indicated that he was unconscious at the time, probably from a dose of Propofol, as was used in the earlier crime.

All-news radio reporter Todd Worlick interrupted the biographical rundown with a bit of information he must have picked up from Armstrong or one of the other detectives.

"Is it true that Jackson had been using websites noted for men connecting with each other for sex?"

The commissioner looked at Lt. Long, the detective chief, and then bluntly said: "Yes."

Questions started flooding from the reporters, all asking different things: Is that tied to his murder? Is this killing related to the others? Is this some kind of copycat killing?

All Donnor could do is say "That's under investigation" over and over again. Finally, Mayor Marcus called an end to the news conference with a final plea to keep reports toned down a bit until police had a better understanding of what was going on.

Kate had a feeling that was not to be. Headlines were popping all over the web.

The surgeon arrived, seemed pleased with Mrs. Cooper's condition and treatment during the hours since she had seen her the night before. She led Kate to her office in another wing of the hospital.

"I have good news," Dr. McCullough said.

She explained how the latest stroke had been caused by the development of a small clot near the larger one that had created the earlier symptoms. Nothing could be done about the older injury, but the new one was small enough that it could be eliminated entirely through surgery, and that would alleviate enough pressure to bring her mother back to her condition prior to recent days.

"The problem is, if we don't operate, she might die. That pressure already is increasing gradually and could speed up."

Kate absorbed the doctor's words with concern and a degree of hope.

"Do you need some sort of consent? Is that what you're looking for from me?"

"Under the conditions of her living will, we could proceed because it is not merely a life-saving procedure but is one intended to enhance her health. I just want you to be aware of all the risks and benefits. The only thing you'll have to sign is an acknowledgement that you received them."

She could tell Kate didn't fully understand.

"If you would like to talk to someone else about it... maybe Barbara?"

In her exhaustion, Kate didn't know what else to do. She knew that Barbara had worked with McCullough and that she would agree with the surgeon.

"No, no, I'll sign." Gathering her thoughts to explain her reluctance. "It's just that... It's been a rough few days."

The doctor smiled softly.

"I understand. Just check at the desk at the end of the hall and they will give you the papers. We will have your mom in at six tomorrow morning for pre-op. The surgery will last between three to five hours."

Kate went back to her mother's room and found that she was sleeping.

"I'll see you early tomorrow morning Mom," she whispered, and then left the hospital.

The wind was beginning to gust and clouds sweeping overhead indicated rain was coming fast. She got in her car and drove east away from the storm, but it was catching up as she arrived at her mother's house.

She took a bottle of water from the fridge and plopped in the recliner where her father once sat, with Kate lodged on the sofa opposite it playing with her dolls. She wondered what he would do, how he would cope with all of this, not just with growing old and infirm but with life in general as it was shaping up in the 21st century. She listened to the rain beat on the roof and watched a trail of water swirl slowly down the picture window in the den, overlooking the gentle slope of the back lawn to the edge of the lagoon.

Then she fell into a deep sleep.

16. Inside Scoop

Paul's text woke her.

"Will your mom have surgery? How is she otherwise? Heard about suspension from The Tide. Come talk?"

It was so unexpected, Kate thought she might be dreaming, yet she was pleased he was reaching out to her for a change. It was dark out. She was still in the recliner. She called him back. He was upstairs at Kevin Barry's Pub, overlooking the river.

By the time she showered and dressed and made it to River Street it was almost 8:30. Mindful of the early morning ahead at the hospital, she climbed the pub stairs and saw Paul at a corner window table, seated across from a woman with long blonde hair.

"Oh, great!" Kate thought as she approached the table.

Midge Cochran was a young cop who had had her eyes on Paul for a long time. Working undercover, she didn't hang out with other officers, but a disgraced ex-cop was OK. She could conveniently pretend that he was only a source. Kate felt that any relationship with Midge was not in her own best interests.

Not that she was jealous. She knew Paul wasn't interested in Midge, but it bothered her that he didn't seem to mind the flirtation.

"Hello, Midge. What brings you here?" she said with a smile and a slight acid twist as she took the open chair next to Paul.

"I ran into your boyfriend after having dinner with a couple of friends."

"And you decided to stay and have drinks. How nice."

"Yeah," Midge said, oblivious to the sarcasm. "We were just

talking about the story that got you canned."

"Well, suspended..." Kate said as she signaled the waitress.

"Whatever. Anyway, that's just one of the crazy things happening these days."

Midge's investigative sources were extensive, through several layers of Savannah society and across cultures on every level, Kate knew. She ordered a fish sandwich, then she and Paul listened intently as the detective rambled on to them about the serial killing investigation, things she had learned from other police officers, prosecutors, and defense lawyers, as well as on the street. Midge got around. She was kind of tipsy, too.

"Did you know they have video? Yes, after the third killing they started using drones with infrared cameras and put up video cameras at all the squares – except Orleans Square," she said with a laugh.

"They figured it was so open that nobody would try to stash a body there. Plus, there were enough other devices around already that somebody assumed they would get something."

"What did they get?" Paul said. So low key. Kate admired his approach to interrogation.

"Well," Midge said, trying to recollect details. "A camera on Hull Street on the northeast corner of the square recorded a man pushing a wheelchair and rolling it into the park at the entrance facing McDonough Street. There's clearly another figure in the wheelchair.

"But, guess what? An infrared camera on a drone passing overhead at the same time shows this figure pushing the wheelchair along the walk. It's obscured by trees, right, but the infrared picks up the heat from his body – but that's all!

"That's right! There's a stiff in the chair!" Midge guffawed as if this was one of the funniest things she had heard.

"Then, a camera picks this guy walking out of the west side of the square onto Barnard Street, carrying the wheelchair folded up. Only, the camera is at the Civic Center a block away. The image is kind of grainy, and the man is clearly in some kind of disguise, but he's obviously not the guy they have in jail."

Midge took another long pull on her beer.

"Why haven't they released the video of the guy going into and out of the park? It might be grainy, but it's got to be of some help," Paul said.

"They are, tomorrow morning. Or maybe tonight, on the 11 o'clock news. That's the only reason I can tell you about it. The infrared thing, though, that's a secret."

They sat in silence mostly for a few minutes, Paul and Midge nursing their drinks and Kate finishing her sandwich, washing it down with a glass of water.

"I'll tell you, though. If you only knew." Midge seemed to be giving an invitation to ask her.

"What else?" Paul said.

"Well, you know that guy? The one they arrested? I don't know what's going to happen to him."

"The latest killing doesn't seem to fit," Paul suggested.

"Well, of course not. Patrick Cummings is still in jail. He didn't kill this guy. And the witness who said Cummings told him he'd killed the other victims, he's the same one who found the body!"

"What?" Kate and Paul both burst out in unison.

"Y'all, this is so messed up," Midge said. "Yeah, they say this guy happens across a body in Franklin Square, then a few hours later when they're questioning him about it, he says, 'By the way, this homeless guy I know told me he's been killing people.' Yeah, right!"

"Then, he shows up on video," Kate added.

"Very convenient, right? And he confesses! Serial killings solved a week before St. Patrick's Day. Like I say, messed up."

"Man, I'd like to talk to that witness and find out what's really going on," Kate said.

"No, you wouldn't," Paul shot back. The women looked at him.

"Kate, remember how you got into the position you're in now. You need to cool it. You don't need to do any more 'investigating' on this one until things cool down with Ted."

Kate felt stung. Midge was looking at her over the rim of her glass with eyes that said: "Whoa! Watch out. Daddy says 'No!'" She was embarrassed at being admonished.

"I don't have to be representing The Tide. There's nothing to stop me as an individual from going around and asking questions."

"No, but it's still not a good idea. At this point, it could be dangerous."

Double sting. Now he was sounding paternalistic. Midge sort of rolled her eyes to the side. Kate was steamed, but she decided to let it go. It was increasingly bothering her that it was getting to be time for her to go and neither her boyfriend nor this other woman showed any signs of leaving.

They paid the tab and moved downstairs. Kate excused herself to go to the restroom, and Midge followed while Paul stood at the bar.

"You know, I can get you to the witness who found Pederall's body and who said Cummings confessed to him," she told Kate after a minute of chit-chat in the ladies room. "I don't know if he'd talk to you, but since you're not going to be writing anything he might be more inclined."

Kate knew there was an angle to this, trying to get closer to Paul through her or something, but she decided to take the chance.

"His name is Curb Washington. He works at the Gator Tail

Grill on MLK, just around the corner of Congress Street a quick walk from Franklin Square. Tell him you talked to me, and at least he might be civil. He knows me."

Kate nodded but didn't say anything. Midge deftly texted her Curb's name, along with a phone number, as a reminder. They rejoined Paul, and it didn't take long before she was sickened by Midge's fawning all over him, as well as his seeming oblivion to it, which only made the display worse. Regrettably, she had to run get some sleep in the hours before the surgery. While Midge was turned talking to the woman next to her at the bar, Kate gave Paul a solid, possessive kiss and whispered in his ear.

"You're not going to sleep with that slut, are you?"

He jerked back surprised, then laughed.

"No, baby. You know you're the only girl for me."

Then he kissed her – in a way that made her feel a part of one again. And that made her feel good.

17. Curb Washington

Kate felt great about her mended relationship with Paul as she left River Street. So, she almost felt guilty just going by the Gator Tail Grill. But after all, it was almost on the way, and it did no harm to drive by the place just to get an idea of what it was like. She had a general idea of the neighborhood of bars, lounges and night clubs that spread west from downtown and over into the burgeoning Canal District, but it was not a place she frequented.

The establishment looked like the type of place real gators would hang out. A small group of skin heads was outside the door smoking cigarettes, laughing, and talking, while a tan pit bull lay unchained under a front window, which had a wooden shutter that was literally falling off its hinges. The paint on the sign over the entrance was faded and chipped, and there was broken glass in the gutter out front.

Despite its name, it wasn't a diner but a bar that just happened to serve some food, mostly buffalo wings, burgers and seafood baskets. People didn't go there to eat; they went to drink or hook up and then move on to some neighboring dive to delve further into the night or to a nearby hotel for intimate companionship.

As Kate was scanning the joint from across the street, a guy walked out the front door who could only be Curb Washington. He was tall and lanky, and he stood looking up and down the sidewalk with an air of both supreme confidence and ultimate caution.

"Curb" Washington got his name working curb service at Carey Hilliard's drive-in on Skidaway Road as a young teen. He also was a basketball star at Johnson High, where he became noted for "curbing" the shooting of opposing teams. Junior college offered him a chance for a way out, but association with crack peddlers and gamblers – lifelong friends – pulled him back down.

His big-time playing days over, Curb confined himself to matches on some of the local courts, but his presence in Municipal Court was frequent. Minor scrapes for assault, driving under the influence and possession with intent had given him some stints in jail. He wasn't working in the Gator Tail kitchen as a career choice.

In short, to Kate's way of thinking Curb – now in his 60s and living on a shoestring — was a likely candidate for a police witness who would say almost anything. And now, if this was the right guy, this was her chance to try to talk to him. It might not come again. Kate pulled closer into a parking space, hopped out of the car, and darted across MLK.

"Are you Curb Washington?"

He wheeled around so fast he almost fell over. But he quickly regained his composure and looked at Kate up and down.

"Well, well. Who wants to know?"

She briefly explained who she was and why she had come, throwing in that she was suspended from her job and would guarantee him that nothing he said would appear in any article.

"I don't even have a notebook on me, much less a recording device."

He looked at her as though she was speaking gibberish and he was having more and more trouble understanding.

"Honey, are you for real? Why would I talk to you, or any reporter?"

She didn't have a convincing argument.

"I guess some reporters want to know things so they can tell everybody else, and some reporters just want to know things. I guess I'm one of those."

He seemed as skeptical as a church deacon asked to take a confession, but then a light went on.

"Oh, I know who you are. You're Paul Camden's girlfriend – the one who writes for that online website."

"Oh, great," Kate thought. "He knows Paul. Now, not only is he not going to talk to me, but he's also going to tell Paul, who'll be mad that I came."

"Look, can't you just fill in a few things for me. I'm trying to piece all this together and could use your help. And don't tell Paul. He didn't want me coming down here."

"He's got that right," Curb said, looking around. The skin heads in front of the Gator Tail had been hooting and gesturing at Kate, and one of them was grabbing his crotch and staggering forward, bow-legged.

"You got a car?"

Kate motioned across the street. They hurried through a break in the traffic.

"I'm off early tonight. Don't want to hang around that place," Curb said, looking back at the bar as they pulled out headed south on MLK.

Kate was moving slowly in case she was going to turn.

"Where're we going?"

"The Purple Peacock. You know where that is?"

"I do." She turned right on Gwinnett Street.

The Purple Peacock was a gay bar in the heart of West Savannah's growing entertainment district. Wedged between downtown and the port, with streets that became thoroughfares to the airport and the boom areas west of the city, it was poised for rapid development over the next decade.

Kate had never been to the Peacock before, but it was a well-known place – famous, in fact, within the gay communities of Atlanta and Jacksonville and Orlando. It was known by a purple neon sign, a peacock with a fantail in shades ranging from lavender to violet.

Inside, rock music was pulsing, lights flashing and people in bright costumes were dancing as though it was Mardi Gras. She and Curb were ushered by a "hostess," who seemed to know Curb, to a table in a far corner away from the bar, where there was an act of three trans dancers in high heels.

Curb gave his order to their usherette, who was a man dressed in a maid's uniform, and then looked blankly at Kate.

"I'm not having anything. I have to get up early tomorrow morning," she said politely.

Curb leaned across the table and looked seriously into her eyes.

"If I'm talking to you, you're having a drink."

Put that way, it didn't seem to be a choice. She ordered a rum and coke. Both Curb and the waiter continued to stare until she pulled a $20 bill from her purse and handed it to him. She didn't expect any change.

Curb didn't have much to say, and Kate wasn't sure what to ask, until their drinks arrived. Mainly, she just gazed out over the crowd of mostly men dancing with each other and having a good time as the DJ played one all-time hit after another. She asked him a couple of times about how he came to find the body and he just shook his head like he couldn't hear her above the music.

The rum and coke was certainly the strongest she had ever had; it seemed as if the bartender had mixed it in reverse proportions. She could only imagine that Curb's martini was just as powerful, if not more so. At any rate, he began to loosen up.

"Yeah, I found that stiff," Curb said. "I'd give anything if I'd never said a thing."

"Why is that?"

"Man, I'm walking out of there, just like always when I don't get off until late. I rounded the corner of Congress Street, cut through the square and – I don't know – you just couldn't miss it.

"I thought about passing right on by. But then I thought: 'Curb baby, as soon as you ignore this thing, the sooner somebody's going to find out you were here, and the cops are going to say you had something to do with it, or otherwise you would have reported it.'

"So, I got on my cell phone and did my civic duty."

He drained the last of the liquid from his glass and started munching on the olive.

"And did doing your civic duty do the trick?"

He looked at her incredulously and laughed.

"Nah, man. That's why you're here."

He motioned with his empty glass that he needed another. The dance floor erupted with some wild rave-type tune. Another waiter, this one carrying a tray of martins, like at a fancy party, stopped by their table, and put a glass down in front of Curb.

"Looks like you're going to need another." She started to take Kate's glass.

Kate pulled it back, but then, observing the look on Curb's face, she relented and said to bring another rum and coke. She pulled out another twenty and watched it vanish from her fingertips. She took the last few sips from her glass and pushed it to the side. Curb was showing signs of nursing his second drink more than the first one. Maybe that meant he was going to loosen up some more and really tell her something.

"So, reporting the body was only the beginning of it?"

He took a long pull from the martini, his eyes staring at her over the rim. He stretched back in his chair, moving his leg close enough to touch hers. She changed positions in her seat to cross her legs away from him.

"No. A little bit later, that afternoon, the cops come to my house..."

"Who?"

"Long. And that guy Armstrong." He sighed, as if recalling a moment in which he wished he had been thinking more clearly.

"What did they say?"

"Oh, they kept saying things like, was I sure I didn't already know the body was there or did somebody tell me it was going to be there. You know, standard stuff..."

"It doesn't sound like standard stuff to me."

"Well, lady, if you lived down here you would think so." He took another drink. "Somebody like me, they're always angling to get something on you, to hold something over you or to blame you for something somebody else did to get them off the hook. You get used to it."

"So, what happened?"

"Well, they're the ones that brought up this guy, this Patrick Cummings. Asking me did I know him, and when was the last time I talked to him."

"What'd you say?"

"Well, as a matter of fact, I had just seen the guy the previous week. I've seen him around for years. He used to hang around the alleys between East Bay and Broughton. I think he's had a place to stay for the past couple of years."

"They say he worked for Frederick Pederall, the guy you found."

"Hmph. Worked for him? If he ever worked for him, it was in his yard or something."

"Pederall lived in an apartment."

"Whatever." Curb motioned for another martini. "I don't know what that means, worked for him."

Kate was sure that she'd had enough to drink. All she had was a ten anyway, but the waiter didn't seem to mind. That was a good thing. She didn't feel like hassling with anyone. Her head was feeling kind of foggy. Curb placed his hand across hers on the tabletop. She jerked back, but it seemed in slow motion. His voice was sort of fading in and out. It was hard to tell what he was saying. The music was rocking the room and rolling the crowd behind her into a tribal frenzy.

Abruptly, it stopped.

"So, how come you got suspended from your job?"

Kate summarized the insubordination rap, and how she felt it was unjust because it was mainly due to her asking around about Lindsey Weatherford and his plans for the Seraphim Society.

"Hmph. Lindsey Weatherford. What a piece of work." His comment seemed to reveal a familiarity beyond just knowing the name.

"You know Lindsey Weatherford?"

Curb's speech was getting slurred. He made a feeble sweeping motion with his martini hand.

"Back in the day, you'd find him here." Kate's eyes followed his hand motioning toward the crowd. "Back before he got big time."

He laughed slightly and nodded slowly at his own words.

"Back then, you'd find Lindsey Weatherford in all the gay bars, from Jacksonville to Charleston. Especially those around Savannah and Hilton Head."

"Lindsey Weatherford is gay?"

Kate felt like she sounded astonished, although it was more like a mere surprising turn of events. Curb nodded assuredly.

"That was before he went all formal. Things got tight in the 80s. Some people changed. He confines all his secret activities to places like Atlanta and New York, or Miami, now. Only word is, he's got a new exclusive hottie lover now right here at home."

The numbness in Kate's legs had extended to the rest of her

body and crept into the back of her head, edging forward with every ticking second. She felt unable to move at all. Whatever Curb was saying, it was sinking in at some level, but she would have to recall it later. His voice drifted in from the top of the ceiling.

"Now me, on the other hand, I can go either way."

He was moving closer, his hands on hers across the tabletop again. His breath was a noxious mix of booze and garlic.

"So, what do you think about this foundation having anything to do with these killings? Or Lindsey Weatherford?"

He leaned back, giving it some inebriated thought.

"I don't know about that." His eyes darted to either side. "Word out here is that the Russian mafia is behind this stuff. Now, how Lindsey could be tied up in that I don't know."

"What could he possibly have to do with the Russian mafia?"

Again, in confidential tones against the noise of the nightclub, Curb said, "Take a look at something called Krimsky Express. It's a shipping company. They have offices here."

He seemed to be getting impatient and anxious again. He lunged forward once more, pulling at her.

"Why are we talking about that. Come on, baby. Let's go somewhere. Your boyfriend doesn't have to know."

The music had started again, boisterously, and a conga line had formed and moved around the room, swinging close to their table. Kate surprised herself by reaching out and taking someone's hand, moving into the line, weaving, and snaking out onto the dance floor. Curb also was up from his chair, glass in hand, dancing toward her.

Then two lines had formed. She was at the rear of one, and Curb led the other, chasing after her line wherever it went. They moved around the room to the beat of the music, and then out the front door and into the parking lot. For a moment, it seemed as though all the dancers had moved through the front seat of her car. And then around the parked cars again, and then up – up over the Purple Peacock and swirling through the air, low overhead the buildings of downtown and out over the islands and sweeping in a wide loop over the ocean before turning and sailing back, racing almost, low over the trees and houses back to the nightclub.

Inside, the dancers moved into one giant line, and off of the floor surrounding the bar and DJ's stand and into a hallway approaching two large doors, which swung open to reveal a cavernous chamber resembling a cathedral of some sort. Kate found herself walking down a long aisle, like a solitary bride, as the music ebbed and flowed into an orchestral cant. All the varied dancers from the club were sitting in the seats, naked, and at the end of the aisle stood a high priest in a tall, jeweled hat.

As she drew nearer – not exactly walking, really, but more sort of floating – she realized that the priest was Lindsey Weatherford. Beside him stood Curb Washington, dressed in jeans but wearing a tuxedo like a groom. She recoiled in horror at the idea of being wed to him.

Suddenly, Kate awoke. She was back in her bed at her mother's house on Wilmington Island. She had no idea how she got there.

18. Meeting Weatherford

It was 6:40 a.m.

Her mother's surgery was supposed to begin at 7:00, and she had instructions to be there at 6:00 to sign the final responsibility documents so preparations for the operation could be made.

Kate quickly called the number on the hospital papers she had and talked to the head nurse. She said she was on her way and was told to relax, that pre-op had already begun as scheduled. She still only had about 15 minutes to get there. Her breath smelled like a cross between the bottom of an old rum barrel and a dumpster, and she didn't have time to even brush her teeth, so she pulled a twig of basil off the plant on the kitchen windowsill to chew on her way.

Kate wasn't sure exactly when her dream began and reality ended, but she was positive that Curb Washington or somebody put something in her drink.

She was equally sure that the part about sailing over Savannah was an illusion. Joining the conga line seemed real enough, although following it out into the parking lot seemed unlikely. And the scene with Lindsey Weatherford acting as a high priest in the back of the Purple Peacock obviously entered her head just before she woke up. She still didn't remember getting to her car and driving home. But her clothes were intact, and no stranger was beside her in bed. That was a good thing.

There were several takeaways from her conversation with Curb. He confirmed her suspicion that the suspect's "confession" was a lie – although for what reason Kate could only speculate. It could be because police were under pressure to have a suspect in custody, to ease fears about a serial killer on the loose just before the biggest crowd of the year was expected for St. Patrick's Day. Or it could be to cover for somebody, for some unknown reason.

On the other hand, other than revelation of Lindsey Weatherford's secret sex life, Curb had nothing to add to the mystery surrounding the billionaire and the murky dealings of the Seraphim Society. The bit about the Russian mafia and its supposed local connection, Krimsky Express, would take some digging. She couldn't do that without further jeopardizing her job. Was it worth it, at this point, to do more to alienate Ted? She needed to talk to Paul. If there was only some way she could do that without him knowing where she had learned the information…

The morning rush was just beginning, so traffic was relatively light going in on Victory Drive and getting on Truman Parkway. It was 7:08 when Kate arrived at the Candler Hospital parking lot. She scanned her teeth in the visor mirror to make sure there were no tiny green basil bits and rushed to the surgery center waiting room. There she learned there had been a slight delay anyway, so her signature arrived just in time.

It was a grueling wait – more than four hours. Most of the time Kate spent sitting in the same chair with her head in her hands. Occasionally, she glanced at her phone to see if there was any news on the serial killings, but there wasn't. All politics and weather. It was already beginning to rain.

Finally, Dr. McCullough came out into the waiting room.

"Everything went OK. Your mom is in recovery now and will be wheeled to her room after lunch. Kate don't expect there to be any difference yet. It will take a few days before we have a good measure of the ultimate success.

"What I can tell you is that the pressure on a critical point has been alleviated. At the least, it should relieve some suffering that your mom has been unable to express."

Kate felt relieved as well. She went to the hospital cafeteria and got a bite for lunch. As she was making her way to a table her phone rang. It was Ted Bridger. She called him back as soon as she had eaten her bowl of tomato soup and a grilled cheese sandwich.

"Kate, good to hear your voice. You sound better, stronger, than when we talked yesterday."

"I'm at the hospital right now. Mom's surgery was this morning."

"Sorry to bother you. I just wanted you to know that something has arisen that might help us both out, as far as your suspension is concerned.

"Lindsey Weatherford's assistant, Mark Blank, called. He said the big man himself would like to talk to us. To 'clear up any misunderstanding,' he said."

"Are you going to talk to him?"

"That's just it. He specifically asked for you. If you can go over there with me, you can ask whatever questions you want – provided they are respectful, of course – and we can both get a feel for whether he's telling the truth."

"Today's just not a very good day."

"Well, it's our only chance. Blank said Weatherford's traveling the rest of the week, and then will be caught up in the parade and party activities for the holiday.

"I'll tell you what I'll do: You can go back on the payroll right away, instead of the earliest being next week. That will help you out with expenses you may have regarding your mother. How is she, by the way?"

The last question, Kate thought, Ted must have felt was obligatory because he was trying to get her to do something. She wanted to tell him he could stuff his offer, but the temptation to actually talk to Lindsey Weatherford was too great. She arranged to meet with Ted at 4:00 at the billionaire's office downtown. She found it telling that it took one billionaire – or near billionaire – to get in to see another one.

By the time she had finished lunch and strolled through the hospital atrium area, where a couple of dozen people sat scattered with phones attached to cradling hands, Kate's mother was back in her room. The nurse told her Mrs. Cooper had been awake in recovery, though not very responsive. Now, she slept again.

Kate sat by her bedside and gently stroked Katherine's hand. The mother-daughter relationship had come full circle. Now, it was she who was dependent, even more so than an infant. And instead of growth, there would only be further regression. Kate longed for an end to this dream as well as the one she'd had earlier, only she knew the end to this one had a finality to it that she was not prepared for.

She called Paul to tell him about her upcoming interview with Lindsey Weatherford. He congratulated her on her persistence and tenacity but told her he felt sure she would get no closer to cracking the case. They arranged to meet later for an early dinner.

Kate left the hospital feeling fairly optimistic. Traffic was light. Rather than the expressway, she took Abercorn and Drayton Streets downtown. Weatherford's office was in an unmarked suite on the fifth floor of a renovated 19th century office building near Wright Square. The only way to get up was to be met by a security guard and escorted on an old wobbly elevator that seemed just as old as the building itself.

As she waited with the security agent, a burly former NFL player named Joe, Kate noticed the office directory posted by the elevator. There on the fourth floor, one level below Weatherford's suite, was a listing for Krimsky Express.

"What is that company?" she asked the guard.

"A shipping company, ma'am."

"Is it Russian?"

"I don't know about that, ma'am."

She expected the lift to let out into an expansive reception room. Instead, there was a carpeted hallway with one door off to either side and one at the end. An extremely lean blonde woman named Jeanine came out of that one and greeted Kate as the security man vanished into the elevator behind her.

Ted was waiting in the next chamber, seated in a leather backed comfort chair. Jeanine immediately opened yet another door, revealing a silver-haired man behind a large desk in front of a palladian window overlooking the square below. He stood at the same time as Ted, and together they were introduced by Jeanine. She asked if she could get anything for anyone, and with no requests told Weatherford she was leaving for the day.

The tycoon was not what Kate had expected. Instead of an international businessman, he came across to her as the head of a local bank. In fact, he was both. Banks, real estate, insurance – these were the mainstays of the Seraphim fortune, which now spread into pharmaceuticals and sophisticated military weaponry.

"Thank you for coming here today. Anytime there is a misunderstanding circulating about me I like to clear it up as soon as possible, and at the source.

"Not that I think that either of you are the source of these nasty rumors swirling around business activities involving the Seraphim Foundation. But surely you see the harm that can be caused by helping to spread them, especially through mass media."

"Why, Mr. Weatherford, as I explained to you before, The Tide has no intention of publishing anything about this," Ted said.

Kate cringed. Her impression was that Ted wouldn't publish anything even it was true, unless it might possibly win a Pulitzer Prize and heap attention on him and his website.

"Be that as it may, I know you realize how sensitive a subject like this is at a time like this. The Seraphim Foundation is amidst a major transition requiring the cooperation of all the proxies involved, and to be linked to a scandal such as serial killings...

"Why, you can imagine how appalling it is to be associated

with such a thing, as untrue as it is."

Kate felt that she needed to take some initiative if she was going to learn anything at all.

"Mr. Weatherford, I am not an investigative reporter, although I guess all of us are by nature, depending on how curious we are. But the fact is, certain questions arose that spiked that curiosity, and the questions involved what appeared to be the only lead in what you have to admit is a huge news story."

"Yes, I suppose it is, however you judge things like that. Sensational, anyway," Weatherford said.

"We are not, you understand, pursuing a story," Kate continued. "Just following leads to help us learn what turns the story might take."

"That sounds like doubletalk to me," the businessman said. "But I'll take your word for it that you didn't intend to write anything. I know that for a fact, anyway, because there was nothing to write. No connection at all."

Ted was about to utter another one of his cringe-worthy comments, but Kate cut him off.

"Perhaps if we had a better understanding about the Seraphim buyout program. That's something that could be helpful from the standpoint of understanding how the rumors originated."

"Well, I've been through this so many times already, with the press as well as lawyers and regulators. But in a nutshell, it's pretty simple. The Seraphim Foundation possesses upwards of a billion dollars in assets that it no longer needs.

"Cash resources and investments alone are enough for the foundation to fulfill all of its obligations for some time to come. Donations received annually will help continue growth.

"Our legal research has shown that the original intent of the foundation's founders was to make use of the assets as long as it was prudent to do so, and then have them returned to private hands. This was considered a burden on the trustees and others who would have to take responsibility for them. Many of these holdings – the real estate, for example – carry significant liabilities, taxes and so forth."

"Are you, personally, taking a tax hit?" Ted asked.

Weatherford seemed surprised by the question.

"No, the tax laws have changed substantially within my lifetime. Let's just say they have changed enough to make undertaking responsibility for these assets – for a man like me – a break-even proposition, more or less."

"Then, how is it good for the foundation?" Kate asked.

"Very simple: administration." Weatherford paused for effect. "When the expense of the business of running a charitable foundation becomes too great, something's wrong. And administration costs of Seraphim are getting out of hand..."

The door cracked open, and a man stuck his head through.

"Uncle Lins, it's almost time to go to the airport."

It was Mark Blank, Weatherford's attorney. Kate recognized him from television reports and news conferences involving the billionaire.

"Sure, sure. We were just finishing up here," Weatherford said. Blank stepped into the office as the tycoon was introducing them. "Mark, here, is my nephew, as well as my attorney. I had wanted him to join us today, but something came up."

"I'm sure you could handle these two, Uncle Lins. They look pretty docile to me, for journalists," Blank said with a chuckle. His uncle and Ted also laughed softly. Kate was observing the dynamics of the room.

It struck her that Blank was a good-looking man, a little older than she. He seemed to recognize her attractiveness as well, but not in a way that made her think he was attracted to her. Meanwhile, she watched as they engaged in small talk with Ted. Something about Weatherford and Blank made her wonder if theirs was more than a business or familial relationship.

"Thank you for meeting with us today," Ted was saying, clearly ready to head out the door. "I think we all have a better understanding of where we're all coming from now."

"We're always open to discuss things that affect our public image," Blank said. "And, as I said, it's best to go straight to the source."

The others were on their feet, so Kate arose from her chair, too. This was the best time as any to ask:

"Are you familiar with a company called Krimsky Express?"

All three of the men seemed taken aback.

"Not really," Weatherford replied. "I think they have an office in this building."

"It's the old K.K. Enterprises run by George Krimsky, Uncle Lins," the lawyer said. "They have some foreign investors now, and they changed the name formally about 10 years ago, before moving in here."

He looked at Ted and Kate as if realizing that explanation might go over their heads. "I don't know anything about them or their current business either," he hastily added.

They said their goodbyes, and Ted and Kate made their way to the lobby.

"What was that all about?" Ted asked when they were outside. "The Krimsky thing?"

"Oh, nothing," Kate said. "I just saw the name on my way into the building and was just curious, that's all."

Ted slowly shook his head. "Well, I hope you got as much out of this as I did. I'm satisfied that there's no way these two are involved in serial murder."

"My impression is the same," Kate said. "But why do you suppose they wanted to meet with us?"

"Maybe they just wanted to size us up? You know, get a sense of whether we're some kind of threat to their business dealings," he said. "There has to be something going on there."

"That explanation of how innocuous it is was not very convincing," she noted.

"I totally agree," Ted said. "But remember, Kate: Leave the investigating to law enforcement."

"That's precisely what I intend to do," she said.

19. Tour of Squares

Since she was sidelined from writing anything, Paul decided it was a good idea to take Kate on a tour of the squares where the bodies were located, to give her a better idea of the grounds for his theory which would rule out sound reason – sanity even – as an ingredient of the motive for the murders.

Cold, dark gray clouds blew in from the west as they set out on bicycles for Crawford Square, on the edge of the Historic District. It was the time of year in Coastal Georgia that winter and spring often shared the same 12-hour span, and a warming sun that poked through the sky intermittently promised there would be more of the latter before the day was out.

"So, what's the significance of this place, again?" Kate asked as they walked their bikes up to the Victorian gazebo where Nancy Janston Oliver's corpse had been found just over three months earlier.

"So, Crawford Square is named for William Harris Crawford, who was a U.S. senator, secretary of the treasury and ambassador to France in the early 19th Century. He ran for president in 1824 but trailed John Quincy Adams and Andrew Jackson in votes.

"Apparently, the killer thought Nancy Oliver was related to the Crawford Ward through a Janston relative whose family lived there after coming to America, but her niece said that wasn't true. Either way, it's evidence that ties into the rest of the picture."

Kate nodded. "I just don't understand how the killer got so close to her and the others in the first place. He had to have known them pretty well for them to have had an element of trust."

"Probably, but not necessarily. He could have posed as a plumber or electrician or something for all we know. I think you're right, though. He knew them and they knew him, probably for some time."

"But why would he want to kill them?"

"That's what we're trying to figure out," Paul said as he glided his bike past the mounded brick cover of an old cistern like those placed in each ward for emergency water supplies after a disastrous fire in 1820.

"Look, this square has a basketball court," Kate noted, glancing over to a pickup game as a neighborhood player hit a three-pointer.

"It's the only one. Just after World War II, an African American basketball team beat other teams from throughout the city in a contest to have it placed here," Paul said. "It's also the only square to remain fenced. The others used to be as a matter of course."

"Probably keeps the basketballs from rolling out into the street, anyway," Kate chuckled as they rode away.

They cut through Colonial Park Cemetery on their way to Oglethorpe Square, which completed the Georgia Colony founder's original concept of six squares when it was laid out in 1742. It was named in General Oglethorpe's honor almost 50 years later after his death.

"I've always thought this was the most serene, pastoral park in the entire city," Paul said as they dismounted to walk their cycles through the shady plaza, covered with tall sweetgum and oak trees on the edge of neatly trimmed lawns dissected by brick walks lined with park benches.

"I haven't really been able to establish a firm link between victim number one and this square, though."

"What do you mean?" Kate said. "I thought you said you had family ties tracing each victim to the square where their body was found?"

"So, I thought I did, but when you try to pin it down, sometimes genealogy and history get murky over a couple of centuries.

For now, I'm satisfied that the killer might have chosen Oglethorpe Square for his first victim as a symbol."

"Sort of like saying, 'I'm going after the entire city"?

"Something like that," Paul said. "Or a certain portion that he feels is represented by the city's earliest memories."

Kate suddenly noticed a black, late model Maxima parked across the square.

"Paul, that looks like the same car that followed me out to Mom's the other day."

He looked toward the vehicle, where the driver in a flat cap stared back for a few seconds before putting the car in motion and slowly winding around the square, then turning a corner and disappearing.

"Am I imagining things, or is that guy following us?" Kate said. "I didn't say anything, but I think I saw him earlier at Crawford Square."

Paul continued his gaze in the direction where the car was headed.

"I think you might be right. Kind of hard to tell for certain." He climbed back on his bike. "As long as he keeps his distance."

She could tell he was more concerned than he let on. As she followed him winding through the ten blocks to Franklin Square, Kate hoped none of this would involve them in violence. She had glimpsed Paul's anger and dreaded what might happen if he felt either one of them was threatened.

They ate pizza at Vinnie Van GoGo's, at the west end of the City Market and looking out over the street at the plaza. Named for Benjamin Franklin, it is one of two squares that have been restored after previously being abandoned to progress. A family of tourists were looking at the Haitian Monument and taking a few photos, while two old men – one in a fez – played checkers at the nearest bench.

"So, what are you thinking," Kate asked. Paul was staring at the opposite corner at the First African Baptist Church, home to one of the earliest black congregations in the United States.

"I'm thinking," he said, turning his eyes to her, "that Frederick Wallace Pederall had more than one link to this place."

"What do you mean?"

"So, his mother was a Wallace, and her family descended from a line of firefighters. An 80-foot water tower stood here when this place was known as Water Tower Square, providing fire protection for the city.

"Not only that, but Pederall might have had ancestors that his upstanding white kin were not all that proud of, if you know what I mean," Paul said, nodding toward the church.

They dropped a few bills and some change on the table for a tip and walked over by the Haitian monument.

"The African American history is rich here in this ward. Franklin Square itself was erased to make way for U.S. 17 in the 20th century, after its water-tower days. After it was restored, this monument, by American sculptor James Mastin, was placed here to honor Haitian soldiers who came here with the French Army to help the colonists try to retake the city from the British.

"That drummer boy is Henri Christophe, who supposedly was among the contingent and later became king of Haiti."

Paul still was drawn to the First African Baptist Church.

"You know, I've always been curious about how the killer got a corpse in here, even at 2:00 or 3:00 a.m. — unless he hid somewhere. That looks like a likely spot."

"What about in a car," Kate said. "Maybe in that parking lot over there. Wait until all's quiet and clear, and then roll by the square and roll out the corpse."

Paul shook his head.

"To me a car doesn't fit this scenario. I picture the dude captured at Orleans Square by the Civic Center camera. Long hair, a hat and coat, he parks not too far away but out of sight. Rolls his victim in his wheelchair, waits over there in the shadows," he motioned toward the church, "and when the time is right, he steers the dead man over by the monument and dumps him, folds up the chair, and exits."

The church had a tall open portico in front up a short flight of steps, so they walked over to see what the view of the square looked like from there. It was possible to see the entire square and at least a block up into the City Market. The killer would be able to detect anyone coming for at least long enough to dump the body.

Paul ran his hand over the iron railing at the top of the concrete steps.

"The police report said they found a trace of fresh blood here the morning Pederall's body was discovered. I haven't been able to learn if they found a match. Or if they also searched inside. I'm sure they must have, but they wouldn't necessarily have to. The killer could have accomplished his end of casing the square right here."

"There's a lot of speculation wrapped up in this, baby," Kate said. "Plus, I don't see what difference it makes if he scouted out the scene from over here or over there." She pointed to nowhere in particular.

"It doesn't, maybe, I'm just trying to get my head inside the mind of a serial killer. How he operates, in every detail, will point us to the suspect. Plus, if he went inside, did he have a key? That opens up a whole new level of possibilities."

They had just stepped down onto the sidewalk when a dark green Chevy sedan pulled up to the curb on the corner. Wills, the detective Kate had seen here at Franklin Square the night all this began, was alone at the wheel. He opened the front passenger window on their side of the car and leaned out.

"Hey, Camden. Come here a minute," the detective said cockily, like a thug in authority.

Paul ambled over 35 to 40 feet and stuck his head through the window. For the next couple of minutes, Kate heard angry voices emanating from the car but couldn't tell what was being said. It sounded like Paul was doing most of the yelling. He stalked back over to her as Wills drove off.

"What was that all about?" Kate asked.

"He asked if we were taking on a police investigation ourselves. I let that go. Then he had the audacity to tell me he has some, quote, friends who are concerned that we might be. I couldn't let that go."

"Friends? What did he mean by that? Is he talking about the police?"

"Considering the context, I kind of doubt it. Anyway, I told him we had already seen one of his friends at Oglethorpe Square. He said, no, that wasn't one of them. I asked him how he knew, and he said he saw him too, because he's following us, too. I really lost it at that. I demanded to know why, and he said, 'Ask my superiors.'"

Kate didn't know whether to be afraid or to laugh.

"Do you think he was telling the truth?"

"If he was," Paul said, "this might open up a whole new can of worms."

20. Unsettling Issues

Kate had two overwhelming tasks to perform: She had to have her mother placed in a nursing home, preferably one with hospice care onsite; and she was compelled to write a puff piece about the beneficence of Lindsey Weatherford, one befitting an archangel.

Since the first hurdle was the only one she considered necessary she spent the next two days researching residential care facilities and narrowing it down to three, one of them in Arlington, Virginia. She visited her mother four times and couldn't tell if she was getting better or if hope clouded her better judgment. During that time, Paul never called, and he texted only twice, to ask her questions about the case and update her on his end. At least he ended each exchange with a heart emoji.

Ted Bridger, on the other hand, wouldn't stop calling, bugging her about the progress of her story on the charitable side of a billionaire who as far as she was concerned might be involved in extortion and murder.

"Mr. Weatherford is a complex man, and this is a complicated story, Ted," she said on his latest call.

"What's complicated about it? You have the data on how much he gives each year and who benefits. Please, just get this job done!"

Kate pictured herself slapping her forehead.

"Well, it's a little difficult to explain to readers how buying up the assets of a charity is going to benefit anyone more than the man himself. I'm still struggling with that part. And you admitted my mom comes first. I'll talk to you later."

At that point she decided all she could do about The Tide was keep stalling Ted until it was no longer necessary, for whatever reason that turned out to be – whether she and Paul left on a sailboat chasing the setting sun or she high-tailed it back to D.C.

She felt finished with Savannah.

A text beeped and she looked back at her phone. It was Paul.

"Know you've been busy but you gotta take a break. Join us at LaFarge's at five. P.S., Midge won't be there."

"Very funny. I'll see you then. P.S, can I bring a date?" she texted back.

Kate turned her attention to appointments for the two Savannah-area residential care facilities she had focused on. The Savannah Senior Towers on the Southside, she knew, was the home of two of her mother's friends, although she was unsure how much interaction her mom needed or would participate in. She was less familiar with her first choice, the newer Senior Sunset on the southwest, marsh side of Tybee Island, which promised many glorious moments as days and lives faded into golden memories.

It was expensive, of course, but her mother was pretty well off, and the sale of her house would bring in enough to keep her comfortable for some time to come.

"Dr. Graf, the director, will be able to see you in the morning. How about ten?" his assistant asked Kate.

"Couldn't be more perfect."

She needed a morning drive out to the beach to clear her head anyway. And she had always wondered about the Senior Sunset, like she had some premonition that her mom would wind up there.

A call to the Towers soon had her another appointment for the next afternoon.

Kate thought it was a good time to do something that would coordinate Ted's interest in Lindsey Weatherford with hers. She couldn't let go of her curiosity about the Krimsky connection.

Curb Washington may be the loser that Paul seemed to think

he was, but he was a wealth of information on other things, such as Lindsey's gay escapades of youth. Could be he knew something about Krimsky as well.

She made a few calls and Susan Jeffries suggested a source she had out at the docks, an accountant for some of the top textile importers who also moonlighted for some fairly disreputable agents.

In no time Kate was showered, dressed in tight blue jeans and a pink sweater, and headed toward town. She texted Paul and told him she was driving out to Garden City to the port and that it was for The Tide's Lindsey Weatherford appeasement story.

She added: "May be a few minutes late to LaFarge's."

"No problem, babe. I'm just rolling back up to the trolley barn now from the last tour. I'll see you when you get there."

The mayor had declared that the St. Patrick's Parade would go off on schedule, so holiday revelers were already arriving and reveling. Kate had to be extra careful with pedestrians. A strange city and drinking too much green beer made for some difficulty, slowing down traffic to a crawl.

Furthermore, the city had to provide enough time for Savannahians to prepare their favorite locations to gather and watch the spectacle. Some had traditional locations along the parade route, either along the sidewalks on Abercorn, Bay, and River streets or in the squares, where they set up chairs, canopies to protect from the bright March sun, and other equipment to enjoy it in comfort.

Normally, they started arriving well before dawn to stake out their claim, but because of the 7:30 p.m. to 7:30 a.m. curfew in the Historic District they were unable to do that on the day of the parade. Instead, they were busying themselves in the afternoon and evenings two days ahead.

It made no sense to Kate because there were plenty of curfew violations on the evening side that the city did nothing about, but she couldn't do anything about it either, so she tried to put it out of her mind as she maneuvered her way through downtown and out

West Bay Street toward the port.

The accountant was a bust. He even seemed amused that she thought he would have anything to share, or that he would share anything if he had such information. At least that would enable her to meet up with Paul on time.

She took Chatham Parkway and the expressway back downtown. After several blocks from the exit onto MLK, then taking Liberty and turning left onto Drayton headed toward the river she had a sense she was being followed. A black limo had been behind her since she was on I-16. That was out of the ordinary.

More out of the ordinary was when she turned again it was still there, through what was now a maze of tourists and vendors hawking balloons, T-shirts, and noisemakers. She called Paul.

"I'm being tailed."

"Are you sure?"

She described the limo, with a driver wearing a cap and a large man in the back seat, also hatted.

"That's strange," Paul said.

"Do you think I should try to lose him?"

"I think your imagination might be getting ahead of you. Go to a public place. Get out of the car and see if you can find out what they want. It could be important to us."

Kate drove to Franklin Square. "Let's see if this rings any bells with them," she thought.

She pulled into a space for horse-drawn tour carriages at the end of the City Market facing the square. There were people everywhere. She got out of her car and the limo pulled up beside it. The rear window lowered, and a loose-jowled man in a homburg and wearing a mustache that could rival a bull walrus said:

"Please get in my car."

"Not for anything, mister!"

"Bah!" Spittle caught in his mustache and on the edge of the window. "I'll talk here."

He told his driver to wait around the corner and got out of the car, a large-shouldered man but one who stood only a couple of inches taller than Kate.

"Why you asking questions about Krimsky Enterprises?"

"Who says I am? And who are you, anyway?"

"I'm Krimsky!" he bellowed, swelling his chest.

Kate was taken aback.

"You're George Krimsky?"

"Yes, and I know who you are," he said in a cross between Russian and Southern American accent. "You're a writer, who writes about murders. I don't know nothing about murders.

"I am honest businessman, and I run honest businesses."

He seemed to be really upset, and he certainly could turn out to be dangerous. She wanted nothing to do with him, and at the same time didn't want to piss him off any further. She invited him to sit down as a nearby sidewalk table was suddenly emptied, even as a carriage had pulled up in a no parking space behind her car and the driver was giving her car an angry look and reaching for his phone to get it towed.

"Look, the story I'm working on has nothing to do with crime," she lied. She gave him a rough idea of the mandate from her boss to chronicle the wondrous Mr. Weatherford, and how she had developed a natural curiosity about Krimsky, an immigrant success story if there ever was one, and the intriguing businessman who was running it today.

He seemed skeptical.

"Well, you can always come and talk to me anytime. Make an

appointment."

"Of course. Maybe after St. Paddy's."

His car had pulled around and the driver opened the back door. Krimsky strode to the car, turned around and pointed his index finger.

"You seem like a nice young lady. But you better not be lying. You make trouble for Krimsky; I make trouble for you."

21. A Sudden Curve

It was 5:30 by the time Kate sat at the small table at their favorite French restaurant. Paul was peering down at his phone but looked up when she pulled out the chair. He immediately rose.

"Wow! You look fantastic!"

"Glad you like me. I'm available if you know anyone I might be interested in," she said as she sat. The remark brought a smile to his face, and his uncharacteristic show of interest in her appearance reassured her that nothing was lost in that aspect of the relationship.

It was going to be a good night, they each concluded separately.

First, they had to produce a little mutual antagonism to make up for later. They did this with their favorite topic of late, the serial murders.

"I just don't see how you can rule out involvement of somebody like Krimsky. The guy's practically a caricature of Russian-Southern Mafia, if there is any such thing."

"Listen," Paul replied, "Krimsky might be involved in a lot of things, but this isn't one of them. There's no motive and no reason to suspect him outside of this vague, supposed connection to Lindsey Weatherford, which appears to exist primarily because they have offices in the same building."

"But Curb Washington said..."

"Curb is an idiot. Not only is he incapable of playing a role in a murder scheme like this – as if he had any reason – he's also not capable of anything unless it's bussing a table. Who would use him for any part of this, even if his role was just playing like he found a body and heard a bum confess?"

Kate had to admit he was right.

"Yeah, he is kind of a loser after all."

Paul tossed her a live one.

"Unless it's persuading young women to go to bars with him."

She blushed. "Oops. You weren't supposed to know about that."

Paul laughed. "Frank Miller told me he saw you. You should have known it would get back. He knew what you were doing there but was still amused to see it."

"Paul, I'm so sorry..."

"Don't be, babe." He took both her hands on the tabletop. "But, Kate," he said, looking deep in her eyes. "You have to be careful. I admire your smarts and determination, but this is serious stuff. I don't want you to be hurt. I love you."

This was what she wanted to hear. She knew it was going to be a better night than either of them imagined.

"So, what do you think," she asked.

Paul reflected for a moment, choosing his words.

"I think we're dealing with a 19th-century family feud." Kate gazed admiring his eyes as much as his intellect. "What started it, I'm not sure.

"But I am sure that at the heart of it we're dealing with a psychopath. To my way of thinking, no one would do this for any reason. But whoever it is exceedingly bright to avoid detection so far. And there is a method to his madness."

The next morning, the method was tested. They were both awakened by Paul's phone. A pal in the First Precinct told him another body had been found, this one in Calhoun Square.

As impossible as it seemed, someone had managed to place a corpse inside a family tent set up for the parade scheduled for the next day. Herbert Pederall, the man Kate had seen at the hospital and who ran away when she tried to question him, was discovered inside the tent sitting in a folding lawn chair. His eyes were wide open, and a note was attached to his lapel.

"Dear Herbert loved a parade. He couldn't wait so he came early."

22. More Connections

Kate was already up and pulling on her jeans. "Can you believe this!"

Paul was observing her, but concentrating more on her hips than what she was saying as she pulled the pants tight against them.

"I can believe the police are unable to figure it out either. Hey, where are you going?"

She was brushing her hair at the bathroom mirror.

"What do you mean, where am I going? I'm going to police headquarters, or Calhoun Square. Somewhere. I've got a job to do."

Paul got up and wrapped his arms around her, looking at her in the eyes reflected in the mirror.

"Kate, Kate, calm down. There's nothing you can do. Nobody's going to let you near the scene, and nobody's going to say any more than the minimum. Believe me, they know nothing we don't already.

"And Ted doesn't even want you to, remember. Not only that, but you've also got to take care of your appointment at Tybee."

She knew he was right. She could accomplish no more today, and probably not over the rest of the weekend. Ted had not actually restored her press pass yet anyway, so nobody was going to let her into a news briefing or near the crime scene.

Paul and Kate dressed and went to get a bite to eat at Bodacious Bagels quietly tucked away on the west end of Jones Street far from the parade route.

"Still, I can't get over the fact that I saw that guy at the hospital, and how scared he was."

She couldn't even tell if he was listening as he stuffed his mouth with an omelet and washed it down with coffee. He took a bite from the biscuit on her plate.

"Paul, don't you think this proves the Seraphim families, as distant as they are, are divided over this billion-dollar transaction."

He took another sip from his mug. "They might be divided alright, but the killer isn't motivated by greed."

"What then?"

"I don't know. But he's clearly a psychopath. That doesn't require a practical motive. And it rules out a hired killer. This one is too erratic."

Kate thought about this for a few minutes as she ate a whole wheat bagel with a slight schmeer.

"But what if there is more than one killer?" she said. "What if the deaths are somehow tit for tat – like in a war over the assets."

Paul considered this for a few seconds. "Maybe, but I don't think so. I think we're dealing with one sick psycho, only I don't know why."

Kate mulled the whole thing over in her mind as she drove out to Tybee Island. This time she took Victory Drive and the Thunderbolt Bridge. She stopped by her mom's off Quarterman and showered and put on fresh clothes and picked up whatever documents she might need.

The ride out over the causeway and through the marsh was pleasant. The spartina was golden, like fields of wheat growing among blue-green streams and tidal pools. The sky was crisp and blue as an October day, and for a while Kate's thoughts drifted away from the murder case.

It was all over the news by now, but she turned off the radio and enjoyed the ride.

After she looked around the Senior Sunset, there was no question left in her mind that that was the place for her mom. It was everything the brochure cracked it up to be. She decided to cancel the appointment on the Southside and immediately began making arrangements to have her mother transferred from the hospital and out to Tybee as early as Monday.

As she was leaving, Kate struck up a conversation with a uniformed security man at the front entrance, Rake Thomas, who was a former cop and an acquaintance of Paul's.

As they chatted, she noticed a white SUV limousine drop off a nicely dressed elderly woman at a circular drive, and she was met by a white-garbed nursing home attendant with a wheelchair. Then the limo circled back by the front entrance and into a parking lot. Kate's jaw dropped when she saw the driver.

"Is that Curb Washington?" she asked.

"Yeah, he gets around doesn't he," Rake said. "He drives part-time for Mr. Lindsey Weatherford."

"WHAT?"

Kate could not help shouting it.

"Yeah. That was Weatherford's mother you saw. She comes once a week to visit her brother who lives here. He's got his own special suite and everything. In fact, I think their family donated the land and put up the money to build this place."

"Really?"

"That's right. Those Pendletons are loaded with cash. They once owned thousands of acres on Whitemarsh and Wilmington islands, and considerable property out here on Tybee."

"Wait a minute. Is that the family of Phineas Pendleton?"

"That's right. Lucy was a Pendleton. Her father, known as 'Penney' Pendleton, made more money from the 1929 Wall Street crash than most people lost altogether. Of course, Jack Weatherford, Lindsey's old man, was already richer than sin when he married

Lucy. That match created a dynasty that could last a hundred years."

"If not forever," Kate said.

Rake got summoned to assist someone in the lobby, and she did her best not to be noticed by Curb as she went to her car and exited the parking lot. He seemed to be absorbed in his phone, anyway, so that wasn't hard.

Kate didn't see Paul that night but had a quiet meal next door at Barbara's and went to bed early like a normal person. Paul called before she turned out the lights and said he was taking his uncle, in his uncle's car, to Brunswick the following day to visit another of his father's siblings and would not be back to Savannah until late the next night.

She told him about seeing Curb Washington driving Mrs. Weatherford.

"Holy mackerel! What comes next out of this?" he said.

"Do you think now you might want to look into what he says?"

"I'm probably more interested in getting my motorcycle fixed. But obviously there is too big of a coincidence here. We have to look into it, but wait until I get back before doing anything, OK?"

"Don't worry. I think I've learned my lesson there," Kate said, not entirely sure she was being truthful.

23. A Promise Broken

Kate stayed away from downtown Savannah the next day as the St. Patrick's Parade, which had been canceled only during wartime and pandemic before, went off without a hitch. Of course, the tens of thousands of spectators lining the parade route didn't mind. Only Calhoun Square was still taped off as a crime scene. Maybe only those who traditionally gathered there for the occasion were the only ones mindful of five people dead and disposed of in ghastly fashion in the middle of the night.

Floats and cars bedecked in green ribbons and sometimes carrying an entire Savannah Irish clan passed by. Sometimes they walked, sometimes they rode fine horses or motorcycles. Bands from schools near and far joined troupes of scouts and acrobats, officials waved as they rode by slowly in backs of convertibles. Stilt walkers carried an Irish flag hoisted so high they had to lower it for power lines along the parade route.

Confederate re-enactors marched as drill teams, occasionally pausing to raise their own stars and bars flag and firing volleys in the air as salutes. One claimed to trace its roots to the actual Civil War and to have been responsible for injecting the Gaelic cry that became the Rebel Yell into the Southern forces everywhere, although there was no way to verify the claim.

Throughout the city, merchants hawked balloons, jewelry and other items from carriages and stands. Beer flowed as freely as the merchandise.

The revelers continued well past dark, filling the bars and restaurants, and restoring normalcy to all except those most obsessed with the killings. It was well past curfew by the time officials had practically cleared the streets of the historic area.

Authorities released no more details on the demise of the latest Pederall, saying that whatever evidence they had gleaned so far could not be released without jeopardizing the investigation.

To Kate, it was a stark situation. The memory of poor Herbert Pederall at the hospital – frightened out of his wits. And nobody seemed eager to do anything to put an end to it, or even be able to do anything.

Finally, Kate convinced herself it was necessary to venture out and do something. The fact that she couldn't tell Paul was a problem because that made it hard to share anything of relevance she might find. She overcame that obstacle by telling herself she was unlikely to come up with anything, but if Curb Washington had anything to do with any of this, other than being unlucky enough to find a dead man, she felt it would be wise to trace his movements just in case.

Hours had passed since the parade by now. She drove into town and took Truman Parkway to DeRenne Avenue so she could enter downtown on the west side of the city along MLK Boulevard. That allowed her to skirt the Historic District and avoid the thick of the curfew. She parked where she had before across the street from the Gator Tail and waited.

Luckily, the wait wasn't long. She saw Curb leaving through the front door about 40 minutes later and headed toward an alley a half block to the south. As soon as he rounded the corner she got out of the car and began following him.

He seemed to know what it took to avoid notice as he briskly skirted through the back streets, now apparently headed all the way across town. Only a few others were out, and twice Kate heard police officers telling stragglers on the sidewalks to move along home. Each time Curb had slowed his pace just enough so that the cops and the partygoers had vanished by the time he crossed a major street.

He wound up at The Pirates' House, a restaurant famed for its ghost stories and tales of unwary young men who in the early days had too much to drink in the tavern and found themselves scooted down a secret tunnel to the wharf below, where they would be impounded to work on a ship. It was said some of them didn't wake up until they were far out to sea and discovered they had new careers as a sailor.

Curb walked around back to a kitchen area, and Kate followed as discreetly as she could, sticking to the shadows and doorways across the street. She saw him talking to two young men, both lithe and dangerous looking. They each held beers in their hands, and the conversation seemed raucous although Kate couldn't discern what was being said. At one point one of the men, who wore a yellow T-shirt and black jeans, seemed to look in the direction where she stood in the darkness of a business driveway. She thought Curb pointed that way, but then his hands were in such busy motion, it was hard to tell.

The three slapped hands and laughed as they broke up whatever bond had held them, and the two acquaintances headed out back around the corner toward the front of the restaurant. Curb lit a cigarette and stood alone smoking for a couple of minutes in the fluorescent light of the restaurant, then also took the direction his two friends had taken. In front of The Pirates' House, he looked both ways, crossed Broad Street at a trot, and headed up the other side toward East Bay Street. The men he had been talking to apparently had gone back inside, so Kate slipped out of her hiding spot and quickly followed Curb as he crossed East Bay and walked into the shadows of the live oaks that line the grassy, parklike area rising above the Savannah riverfront.

"Whoa, bitch!" The youth in the yellow T-shirt suddenly stood in her path. Just behind him, the other character, in a black ballcap, emerged from behind another tree. "Why're you following Curb Washington, bitch?"

The one in the cap pulled out a switchblade and clicked it open into operable mode.

Kate was frozen, unable to speak or move. She heard some commotion behind her and saw a startled look on the two men's faces. She turned and saw Detective Wills running across East Bay in their direction, with his weapon drawn and shouting, "Hold it right there!"

The dude in the yellow shirt turned and ran back into the shadows. The one holding the knife grabbed Kate and held her tightly with his right arm, the blade menacing her face from his left hand, as if he was ready to go into a standoff. Wills halted, aimed his weapon, and made it clear he would shoot. The thug thought twice about challenging the officer, then also turned and ran. Wills let them go.

"Are you alright," he said as he ran up to Kate. She was trembling and didn't even mind as he wrapped an arm around her shoulder. He was on his radio right away, calling Armstrong to tell him what happened. He led her to a nearby park bench and went back over into the trees with a flashlight to make sure the two men had cleared the scene. Kate called Paul and learned he had just arrived back in town.

In about three minutes, Armstrong and Lieutenant Long arrived.

"Alright, let's hear it," Long said, directing the statement at Wills.

"She was following somebody on foot," the detective said. "I don't know who. She started out on Martin Luther King and came all the way over here to The Pirates' House. She ducked in an alley in the back, waited a few minutes. Some men came around to the front of the restaurant, blended with the crowd 'til I lost them. Then she came around and headed over here, where she was accosted by two men, one with a switchblade. I arrived; they ran."

Long turned to Kate.

"Who were you following?"

"Curb Washington," she said sheepishly.

"Go pick him up," he instructed his two detectives. Wills took off on a run to get his car.

"Little lady, you're not even supposed to be out here, much less trailing a person of interest in a murder case."

She was still in shock. She tried to say something but couldn't. About that time Paul arrived in his uncle's car, the old man still sitting in the front seat. She quickly explained what had happened. He was furious – not at Kate but at the police.

"You're still following her?" he shouted at Armstrong. "You have no right. I warned you about this!"

Before the sergeant could reply, Long interjected: "Camden, you've got a big mouth. Wills saved her life. Your problem is you were never the cop you hoped to be, so you keep trying. Now take your girl and get out of here."

Wills had just pulled up to the curb to pick up Armstrong and go arrest Curb Washington. "You want a report on this, lieutenant?"

"What do you think?" Long said as he climbed in his car and drove off.

Armstrong used the opportunity to get in a final word.

"It's not what you think, Camden. We aren't following her because we think she did something wrong."

They both looked at him,

"We think she might lead us to the killer."

The sergeant went off with Wills, presumably to lock up Curb Washington, for at least long enough for him to tell them who the two thugs were who accosted Kate. They obviously didn't think he was involved in the murders either.

Paul took Kate to get her car, with Uncle Roy riding along in his own front seat and her in the back.

"I guess there's no use in saying, 'What were you thinking?'" Paul ventured, glaring at her in the rear-view mirror like a parent who had just realized the kid was out of control.

"No, you can pretty well skip that," she said as he turned onto MLK. They sat in silence for the next couple of blocks until he pulled up behind her car and she started getting out.

"All I can say is, it seemed like a good idea at the time."

He reached back and clutched her hand, which was reaching out to his at the same moment.

"It's a good idea if you stay at my place tonight. Follow me to Uncle Roy's and then we'll go there."

"I wouldn't have it any other way."

As it turned out, it was a good thing Kate stayed downtown.

About 3:00 a.m. that morning, just as another St. Patrick's Day had faded quietly into history, the Historic District bathed in calm again, a sixth murder victim turned up in Warren Square.

24. An Old Score

At 2:34 a.m. a dark gray antique F150 pickup with a rusty hood pulled out of the parking garage next to the square. It went straight up the sidewalk into the heart of the park and stopped. The driver got out, head obscured by a hoodie, and pulled a wooden crate out of the back of the truck, then drove off in the direction of the river just three blocks away. Inside the pine box police found a corpse that the coroner described as mummified.

There were few witnesses because of the curfew. The only people out were drifters who had little to lose by being picked up by the police. The F150 was traced by cameras until it was lost headed east on Islands Expressway.

Still, it was hard to believe that anyone could pull off such a stunt with the massive security presence due to the parade and serial murders occurring downtown. For that reason alone, city officials were not eager to advertise the crime. But they prepared for a media onslaught by quickly holding a news conference to get out front.

"The pickup truck in question has not been registered to anyone for 31 years," Lieutenant Long told the assembled media crowd, which numbered more than three dozen including a few out-of-towners who had come for the parade and stayed for the murder.

"How was an ancient, rusting vehicle able to be parked in a downtown garage for – how many days was it – amid the current crisis?" asked a reporter for the Charleston News & Courier.

"Everyone who saw it assumed it was part of the St. Patrick's festivities," Long said. "Even the head cashier at the garage thought that because the person assigned the space rides in the parade in an old truck each year. It turned out that person is either out of town or in the hospital, we're not sure."

Kate and Paul were watching the press briefing on television.

"Now, that's interesting," Kate said. "I wonder how many of them have crates with a body in back."

Just then, a reporter for the Morning News was asking who held the space.

"We're not at liberty to say at this time," Long said. "We do know they were not involved in the crime, but we believe the killer might have known the individual."

Several reporters were calling out for attention at once, asking the identity of the victim and whether there were any suspects.

"The victim has not been identified at this time. We have reason to believe, naturally, that this death might be related to other homicides that have plagued our city going back almost a year. We have formed a list of missing persons who could fit the profile of other victims in these killings, and through accumulated evidence including DNA we are trying to find a match with the latest victim.

"And, as you might imagine, until we can fit this victim with a pattern, we are unable at this time to name persons of interest."

"Persons?" said Marguerite Williams of Channel 16, seizing on Long's use of the plural.

"Person or persons," Long quickly clarified. "What I can tell you is that recent developments have led us closer to the killer. That's all I have at this time. Information regarding this crime, and the entire investigation into the Square Murders, will be released as soon as it's available."

He turned to go but answered one last question. Todd Worlick wanted to know if the driver of the F150 at Warren Square resembled the person seen dumping a corpse in Orleans Square.

"Based on one angle from one of the cameras, we believe that it was," Long said.

Kate turned to Paul.

"So, what do you make of it all?"

"A couple of things," he said. "We know it wasn't Curb Washington or his friends. They're in jail."

"Ha, ha," Kate responded. "Well, I never would have thought that they did, Smarty."

"The other thing is," he continued, "it appears that the killer is really running out of options. He's close to the end game now. The fact that this victim is in a mummified state means he or she was probably killed before the first Square Murders body was found.

"That indicates that the murderer might have run out of other victims and is wrapping up his work by getting rid of the first."

"But why," an exasperated Kate said. "Why go to all this trouble, and time and effort, and hurting people? Taking their lives for God's sake!"

"It's hard to say with a deranged mind. I guess there's something in there somewhere. Something makes sense to him, and something's telling him he's running out of time to accomplish his final task."

"So, what can that be?"

"We might not know until after it's over. Hopefully, if another death is involved, it will be before that."

Kate got a text from Ted Bridger, imploring her to write up the story on the sixth murder victim for The Tide.

"I know you're technically under suspension. I'll just pay you a bonus. How about a thousand dollars? Please, Kate, nobody on the staff can write this story like you."

She agreed to do it, then immediately regretted it when Ted added: "Of course, don't go off into your theories about Mr. Weatherford. That's a separate story, you understand."

"Yes, Ted. Yes, I understand. Don't worry," she said, rolling her eyes.

"Can you believe that guy?" she said. "Asking you for a favor and insulting you at the same time. How'd he ever get rich."

"They're all the same," Paul said. "If you're going to be writing, I'm going to work out."

He headed out to the gym, and Kate took out her laptop and began pounding out the story of the Warren Square incident, using Lt. Long's briefing to segue into the serial killings background.

She texted Sgt. Armstrong to see if she could get anything new out of him. He called back in five minutes.

"Strictly not for attribution," Armstrong said. "You can check it with Martha Orlando if you need that. The corpse in the crate has been identified as Ella Trask Manchion, who disappeared three years ago at the age of 65. At the time, the person of interest was a guy named Stephen Marks, who had been her on and off boyfriend for decades and disappeared about the same time.

"There was not a lot about it in the media at the time. But there was plenty of gossip and rumors about it in the circles they ran in.

"Seraphim circles?" Kate offered.

"There you go again. You've just got the Seraphim Society on the brain," Kate. "What's the matter, you can't tie this one to Lindsey Weatherford? But yeah, to answer your question, those were the sort of circles they ran in."

She assured him that for the article she was writing for The Tide there was no way that she would even hint that Lindsey Weatherford was still alive.

"Another thing, Kate," Armstrong said. "We had to let Curb Washington go."

"Oh?"

"Yeah, he denied telling those two anything about you. Said he didn't even know you were following him. They back him up. They said you just happened to walk into the park where they were, and they intended to rob you."

"Holy cow, do you believe that?"

"No, of course not. But what are you gonna do? At least they'll be locked away for a while."

"Do you think Curb has anything to do with all this?"

Armstrong sighed.

"I hate to disappoint you, but no. I think you'll soon see, along with everybody else, that this whole scenario you've invented about Lindsey Weatherford and the Seraphim Society is a dry trail."

Kate felt the burning sensation of being told she was wrong.

"And I'm telling you that secretly knowing something that would make you double up on your theory."

"And what's that?"

"The parking garage space where that F150 sat for days next to Warren Square belongs to Mark Blank, Mr. Weatherford's nephew and attorney."

"What? And you still don't consider this a line of investigation?"

"Quite simple, Kate. We've investigated, along with the FBI. There's no evidence of anything like that happening. Ask your boyfriend."

Soon, they would all have reason to retest Kate's theories.

25. A Bold Blunder

It was around 7:30 the next morning that Kate got a call from Todd Worlick, asking if she had heard anything about an attempt to murder one Lindsey Weatherford. He knew nothing more.

Paul immediately texted his friend in the precinct, just a question mark; he'd know what it meant.

He called right back.

"Something is definitely amiss, but he can't say for sure it's the Weatherford thing," Paul told Kate. "But the mayor's supposed to make an announcement anytime now."

"Naturally," she said. "Just in time for network news during a break in the NCAA playoffs."

Soon, the mayor was on the air announcing the "horrific crime practically on the doorstep of the intended victim, one of the most prominent and distinguished residents the city has ever known."

"Not to mention, the richest," Kate laughed. "You'll notice that because there's no obvious link to the other killings he's not about to go there."

"No, of course not," Paul said. "And he's not going to be taking questions. People will draw their own conclusions, though. Just like us."

One positive result of the mayor's statement was that anyone who had any information felt freer to share it now that the attempted murder was out in the open.

"Here's the deal," Paul said after a flurry of emails, texts, and phone calls.

"Only his closest associates knew it, but Lindsey had a young gay lover."

"Bet Curb Washington knew it," Kate interjected.

"Whatever... Anyway, the guy, a hot 28-year-old Haitian named Remy St. Clair, called Weatherford around midnight, and said he was in the courtyard in the back of Lindsey's mansion on Whitaker Street. He asked him to come down, and when he looked out the window Lindsey could see Remy, who appeared to be alone.

"Without saying anything to his security staff, considering the personal nature of the visit, Weatherford went downstairs, despite it being highly unusual as well. When he approached Remy, a man in sunglasses, a face mask and wearing a hat covering a mop of stringy hair came out of the shadows pointing a gun.

"Now, this is the critical part. This man resembled the suspect seen in the F150 yesterday and around Orleans Square the time the fourth victim was found. You know, the diversion killing."

"Oh, yeah. Creepy!"

"But before he could shoot Lindsey, or abduct him or whatever he had in mind, one of Weatherford's security agents opened the electronic gate in the back and entered walking through the drive. It startled the gunman, and Lindsey broke for the back door. The security man drew his weapon, but the intruder grabbed Remy and held his gun to his head, backed out of the driveway and then ran so quickly that he vanished around the corner and down one of several nearby alleys before Weatherford's man could fire a shot. A thorough search of the area turned up nothing."

"Wow! What a story!" Kate gasped. "Can you imagine the headlines this is going to get?"

As if on cue Ted Bridger called, begging Kate to come into the office and supervise coverage of the latest break.

"Of course, I would, Ted, but remember, I have to check my mother into the Sunset out on Tybee this morning."

He promised her another thousand dollars just to come in for a couple of hours and put the whole thing into context for The Tide's readers – "as long as the victim in this case doesn't wind up the villain."

It was too late for that. Online comments on all the stories and memes involving the case painted it as a case of revenge in which people were being offed as a result of Weatherford's business dealings and somebody decided it was time for turnabout. Twitter was especially vicious, as Weatherford had a large following for publicity purposes.

It was the same on the radio, no matter what channel or podcasts you turned to. And it was all the talk at the hospital among the staff and patients, and at the retirement home when Kate arrived with her mother.

"Can you believe this turn," Rake Thomas said as Kate passed him going in. "I'm beginning to think ole Curb Washington might have something to do with this after all."

She stifled a laugh and then said, "I think a lot of people are going to be thinking twice about that."

Katherine was exhausted by the time Kate got her into her room. As a new arrival, she was served a light brunch, and then with the aid of a staff member who would be one of her mom's helpmates for the rest of this life, Kate got her changed and put her in bed.

Kate stroked her mother's hair gently, thinking of all the times the caresses went the other way. She kissed her on the forehead and then slipped quietly out of the darkness of the room and headed back to Savannah.

She spent the next several hours working with The Tide staff to turn out the best story they could under the circumstances, and also arguing with Ted about the necessity of explaining something about the Seraphim Society and the other deaths in order to put the Weatherford assault in context.

It was necessary to go back out to her mother's house, so she stopped by Paul's on the way and told him all about the buzz throughout the city and a global online reach.

Paul smiled at her enthusiasm.

"Yes, but there's more. There's the answer to the whole mystery. I think I have it. And I think I can find the killer."

He got up and walked over to the shelves where he kept scores of books and bundles of documents stacked in moving boxes containing minute details of Savannah's history. He took a folder and plopped it on the bed between them, where contents of old news clippings and yellowed notes spilled out on the spread.

"What if Lindsey Weatherford was the only intended primary victim all along?"

"What do you mean? Oh, the Haitian Monument! What if it wasn't Franklin Square but the Haitian Monument that was important, because of Remy?" Kate ventured.

"Well, I hadn't thought of that, but who knows? What I'm getting at though, is a whole different story."

He showed her some of the old clippings, which reported on big business and scandal at the turn of the Twentieth Century.

"The idea of converting assets of the Seraphim Corporation into those of a charitable foundation belonged to an outsider named Oskar Rosenkrantz," Paul said. "He was a financier from Brussels who married a Lance, an early Georgia family and proud of its proper Episcopal heritage and its good works through things like the corporation was used to doing. He rose to become the president of the corporation.

"Even though he was a Jew, Rosenkrantz was accepted warmly by all the Lances and most of the people in Savannah society. However, there were a few holdouts who cared only that he was a brilliant businessman.

"They rallied to his vision of hiding assets to avoid taxes and other shrewd schemes of his. The conflict came when it came time to share the cream that flowed off the top of the plan. Rosenkrantz and a couple of other key figures from Irish and German Catholic clans involved favored a more equitable approach, while Weatherford's direct ancestors, including Phineas Pendleton, led the majority of the board, which concocted a scheme in which they would profit immensely, and others almost not at all.

"They didn't get all they wanted. Remember, the Society still has vast holdings including thousands of acres of coastal Georgia property which Weatherford is trying to corner today."

Kate had listened with great interest.

"But what does this have to do with the murders?"

"I think the killer's motive is revenge."

"What do you mean?"

"Well, as the process of folding the corporate assets into the foundation proceeded, Rosenkrantz continued to remain an obstacle to doing it the way the ones in control wanted. They decided to get rid of him, in a manner that befitted the Victorian days in which they had thrived.

"Someone created some false documents that pointed the finger at Rosenkrantz as the one who was trying to corner assets for himself. He was arrested and convicted of financial fraud, and his family was ruined."

Kate was stunned by the narrative.

"You think someone today still holds a grudge? Paul, this is one of the best stories I've ever heard. You have to pin it down and let me write it. This could blow the top off the whole city, not to mention Lindsey's scheme to add another billion to his portfolio."

"I'm not there yet. I have to figure out who was affected and who is still around today. I'm thinking maybe someone whose parents or grandparents left the city, and he later returned seeking twisted justice for his family.

"I know you're ready to head back to Tybee to see Katherine first thing tomorrow morning so we'll try doing whatever we can to come up with answers. I'll let you know.

"I'd love to get Frank over, too. He might have a line on this. The man never answers his telephone at home, his voice mail is full, and he doesn't even have a cell phone."

Kate was putting on her jacket for the cool night air.

"He lives in Thunderbolt, doesn't he? I can easily stop by his house and tell him to call you. Or leave him a note."

"Would you, babe? Here's his address on Shell Road."

He shared it to her phone. She gave him a lingering kiss and then was away.

26. Pulling the Weeds

Frank Miller lived in a two-story wood frame bungalow surrounded by trees and shrubs that gave it a cavernous look, with branches swathed with wisteria and jasmine arching over the roof. Paul had told Kate that Frank's folks once operated an antiques business, and the century-old home seemed to fit the family image.

She parked out front on Shell Road, stuffing her bags low in the floorboard and sticking her phone in the back pocket of her jeans as she got out of the car. She was careful to put it on "silent," mindful of Frank's aversion to ringing phones. The wide concrete walkway, dimly lit by a streetlight on a nearby corner, was cracked and broken in many places, with clumps of dandelions growing in patches here and there. Near the steps to the porch was a small pile of wilted weeds and a garden tool, making Kate think of her dad's never-ending battle against aggressive plant life in his driveway.

She felt like a kid approaching a haunted house on Halloween as she trod up the steps and rang the bell by a massive door made from one slab of oak. Through a tiny window she saw there was a light on down the hallway, but nobody was coming, so Kate walked around the corner of the porch and saw a vehicle in the driveway in back. She gave the bell another jab, and through the window saw new light toward the rear of the entrance hall.

Frank came swiftly and looked out and saw that it was her. He cracked open the door, enough that she could see that the hallway behind him was lined with clocks — grandfather clocks, cuckoo clocks, and a variety of others floor to ceiling on either side, creating a narrow tunnel leading to the back of the house.

"Kate! What brings you here?" He seemed as annoyed as he was surprised.

"I'm sorry to disturb you, Frank. Something's come up that we thought you could help us with. Paul said you don't use the phone much, and I was heading out to my mom's on Wilmington Island so we thought I should stop by...

"That is, Paul said it would probably be alright, so if it's not, tell me..."

His stare seemed to say, "Get to the point," so she briefly explained the new theory. He nodded knowingly as she got to the end.

"Maybe you should come in." He cracked the door open wider and looked both ways up and down the street. She felt her phone vibrating in the back pocket as she stepped inside and told herself to check it in a minute in case it was Paul with new information.

Beyond the slim corridor swallowed by timepieces Kate could see into the parlor off to the left. There were two grand pianos stuffed in there, and an upright against the wall.

The stairway leading to the second story also had stacks of antique chairs on each step, and the landing was covered with two roll top desks and other furniture.

"I don't get many visitors," Frank said as they wound their way through the narrow path toward the back of the house. "I always use the back entrance."

"Paul told me your family was in antiques. Looks like you've maintained the tradition."

"The problem is, they learned you can't sell everything," Frank said wistfully.

"Unfortunately, I was never able to get rid of anything either. This whole house is this way, with some of the finest antiques in the South."

He led them into a large room, maybe a dining room at one time. There were several cardboard boxes and a pine crate stacked along one wall, and an elaborately carved four-poster bed in the center neatly made and topped with a cotton quilt.

"I sleep here," Frank said. "You are the only other human who has been in this room since my mother died in 1983."

It was an astonishing realization: strange, and sad at the same time. Kate suddenly felt very sorry for Frank, but unease was also welling within her.

She turned and saw behind her a late 19th century dresser, with a mirror and makeup, and wigs like one would expect backstage in a theater. Folded underneath the table was a fold-out wheelchair.

She was about to say something when she turned around and Frank was holding what looked like a Ruger automatic. It wasn't pointed at her, but its size and his menacing look were enough to chill her to the core. A surge of anger and hatred reddened his face and dilated his eyes to black holes.

"I'm sorry you and Paul had to find out. And I'm sorry you came here, Kate."

Her heart was drumming double time. The gun took on an even larger appearance as he raised it in her direction.

"If anyone figured it out, it would have to be Paul."

Just as Frank said the name, her phone started vibrating again and she knew it was him. If she could just hold on long enough, Paul would come. She had to stall Frank just long enough.

"I don't know what you plan, but Paul knows I'm here. If he doesn't hear from me in a while, he's going to come looking."

"You won't be here. Neither will I. If he sent you, he has no suspicion of me. I'll say you never came."

"Are you going to shoot me? There's no way you could get rid of the evidence."

"No, that's true." Frank said. "Naturally, I'd rather not shoot you. That's messy. But I will. We're going to take a little ride. I'll take care of you, and if I have to, I'll take care of Paul."

"Why're you doing this? Why would you kill those people?"

"You know the answer to that. They ruined my life."

"But THEY didn't ruin your life. Their ancestors might have done some things that did – in a way – but not these people."

She was thinking back to a psychology course on criminal behavior, trying to be the "sympathetic victim."

"It's natural you should feel the way you do. Your people were wronged. But that was way in the past. You can let it go."

"You don't understand. They were always there. My family floundered after my great-grandfather died. I know my family tree. All my life, I've had to watch as these people lived idly in their ill-gotten, inherited wealth and property."

"But that's not their fault…"

"But they're nothing but slugs, and they deserve to die for that alone," Frank screamed. Kate knew she was not going to get through with reason.

"These slimy, creepy slugs. I knew them. I'm ten times smarter than any of them. And with the right schools, the right social setting, I would have flourished among them. Instead, my people have always had to eke out a living, while these slugs just wallow in their wealth, with nothing to show for them being on this Earth, one generation after the next."

Then he delved into what must be his strongest condemnation.

"They're like dandelions – weeds taking up the ground, water and sunlight of more deserving plants."

Kate recalled the weed-picking on the walk and concluded that Frank was stark-raving mad. It was just like Paul said: a psychopathic killer with his own deranged method, carrying out what he perceived as justice through a sick mind looking out at a sick world.

"It was only a matter of getting close enough to develop a trust.

You, as a reporter, are aware of the importance of that," Frank said. "The choice of death was mainly a matter of convenience."

"But you slipped up. The squares were a nice touch, but that will be your undoing. We figured it out, so will the cops."

"Nonsense," he shouted, Kate thought loud enough certainly to be heard outside. "They're not capable of putting this together. They don't have Paul's brains."

She was looking him over, sizing him up. He wasn't much bigger. If she could only get that gun out of his hands...

"Come on, this way." He leaned back against a stack of boxes and motioned with the pistol toward the door. As she brushed past him, she grabbed his arm at the wrist with both hands and pushed it up in the air. He was stronger than she thought. She tried to knee him in the crotch, but his hip turned just in time to deflect the blow. He was quickly able to wrest his arm free and slammed the gun across the back of her head as he brought it down.

The lights went out momentarily, and she fell to the floor. Groggily, she raised her head and felt her hair being pulled hard.

"Get up," he commanded, dragging her to her feet and pushing her down another narrow hall toward the kitchen area of the house.

She stumbled as he pushed her through the back doorway and down the steps from the stoop to the drive. At the bottom of the stairs, he pulled her up again and half dragged her by the arm to the back of an old Chevy coupe. He opened the trunk and pulled out some paint cans and put them on the edge of the drive.

"Get in."

Kate stood teetering over the car trunk, her head pounding and aching where he had struck her and pulled at her hair, which was wet in back, she guessed from blood. Barely able to stand, she leaned over into the trunk and curled up as Frank took her legs and folded them over inside it. He slammed the trunk door, and she could hear the engine start and rumble for a couple of minutes, followed by the car door being opened and shut as if he had gone back into the house.

Simultaneously, she felt a click in her hip pocket. That meant she had a message from Paul. "Please, God, please let him hurry."

27. Relative Revelation

Kate had not been gone more than half an hour when Howell Barker stopped by Paul's to work on some anti-hacking software they were trying to develop. After the usual idle chit-chat, Paul told him about the latest discovery involving family heritage, wrapped in scandal and ruin, and juxtaposed with the squares where the murder victims were found.

"Kate's stopping by Frank's house in Thunderbolt on her way out to her mom's. We wanted to see what he thought about this latest angle – coincidence or deliberate irony?"

"Well, he would know. That's his family."

Paul nodded with the self-assurance of someone hearing affirmation after a period of doubt. Then Howell's words struck a little closer to home.

"Family? What do you mean his family?"

"Oh yeah, I thought you knew that and that's what you were talking about. Oskar Rosenkrantz was Frank's great-grandfather."

Paul was rapidly sorting this new information.

"His great-grandmother was a Lance, and an only child. She met Rosenkrantz on a trip to Europe and he came to Savannah and married her. He was a brilliant businessman and soon was running the whole Seraphim thing, up until the split-up, that is."

"If Frank knew about all this, why hasn't he said something?" Paul said.

Howell could only look blankly back at him as both of them reached a rapid conclusion: It was now apparent that Kate could be in grave danger.

"Could Frank be mixed up in this?" Howell said. "Surely not."

It seemed impossible. Frank was so quiet and withdrawn, he didn't seem to be the type that would want to get involved with other people to even get close enough to kill them. It was one of those situations where you get a wild idea, and it takes a minute or two for the facts to assimilate.

"She only left maybe 20 or 25 minutes ago. Maybe she's not there yet," Paul said, simultaneously calling her. No answer.

"She's not answering. Maybe he wasn't there, and she went on out to her mother's."

Howell nodded. "Give her another minute. There has to be an explanation."

He sat down at Paul's computer and began the process of logging in and calling up the work they had started. Paul was calculating in his head the distances involved – from his apartment to Thunderbolt, Thunderbolt to Quarterman on Wilmington Island. Was there anywhere else she could have gone? The supermarket maybe?

He tried her number again.

"That does it. I'm calling the cops."

To Paul's dismay, Armstrong answered the Detectives Bureau phone.

"Just the person I wanted to talk to, Paul Camden," the detective said with heavy sarcasm.

"I'm not exactly dying to talk to you, but here goes," Paul said.

He quickly ran through the premise of the murders and explained how Kate had gone to Frank's, who – get this – could be involved.

"Frank Miller? You gotta be kidding. I know that guy, he's not capable of killing anybody. Why, Kate could handle him."

"Would you stop and listen to what I'm telling you," Paul said. "We've all had it all wrong. Kate's life is in danger if he's a killer, no matter what."

Armstrong thought for a second. "You could have a case, but we don't know that she even went to his house. Have you gone by there?"

"No, but I will right now. Can you get a squad car to meet me?"

"Thunderbolt's a separate jurisdiction. You go ahead and call me back as soon as you get there. At this point we don't know if anybody's there, including Miller."

Paul threw on a pair of pants and his shoes. With no car and the Harley barely running again, he had to catch a taxi to Thunderbolt. He gave Kate's phone number to Howell and asked him to keep trying it – and to try to get a bead on where the phone was geographically.

Kate's head was throbbing, and her shoulder was cramped and sore from falling and Frank jamming her into his car trunk. There was no emergency latch -- rather, there was one, but it was broken. She wasn't sure, exactly, how long she had been there, but it seemed longer than a few minutes. A strong scent of paint thinner emitted from a rag that lay near her face. She struggled to keep her head clear long enough to think what to do.

Frank had left the vehicle at one point. Of that much, she was sure. She remembered hearing him muttering as he walked away. She had no idea whether he had returned. He could be sitting in the front seat. Her phone was clutched in her left hand, which was cramped up under her chest.

She remembered now. She had managed to wrangle it out of her right hip pocket by twisting her left arm back in just the right position. That was after the device quivered for the third time in a row with God only knew what information that could keep her alive. After that she passed out.

She took a chance on the light from the phone. It was 10:01.

Good. That meant she must have been out only a few minutes. They were probably still at Frank's house. She saw she had two missed calls from Paul and three in a row from a number she didn't know. She made sure the device remained on silent and the volume of an incoming call would be muted in case she had to answer it without making any noise.

She detected sounds of him coming back. She clutched the phone close to her chest, lest the tiniest speck of light creep through a crack in the trunk cover.

The driver's door shut again, and the car started backing out. Frank took Mechanics Avenue across Victory Drive to Bonaventure Road, a curvy trail that served as a handy shortcut from Thunderbolt to downtown.

Kate winced at the odor of the trunk, now also being filled with carbon monoxide each time the car stopped at a traffic signal. It was not as bad when there was movement. Between two of the stops, she had a call. This time she answered it. It was completely silent, and at least she would be on a line if Paul or anybody tried to track it.

She detected the characteristic lingering smell of pizza, popcorn and pralines near City Market, and the bumpy cobblestones of a steep ramp way by City Hall leading down to River Street.

After what seemed like maybe 10 more minutes, they were going down a grade, then around a sharp curve and up a long and fairly steep incline. She realized they were on the access ramp to the Talmadge Bridge over the Savannah River. That meant they were heading to Hutchinson Island, across the south river channel from downtown and into South Carolina.

Frank's house was dark and foreboding when Paul arrived. He saw Kate's car parked in front and rang and knocked at the door, went around back, and noticed a patch of blood on the stair rail. The back door was opened, so he stepped inside and called out: "Kate!"

Amazed at the tomb-like appearance of the place, he nevertheless noticed that the back room seemed in disarray. He saw the makeup table and called Armstrong right away to tell him what he had found.

"Well, what's your sense of it? If he had harmed her, wouldn't they still be there? There hasn't been time for much to happen..."

"Hold on a minute, Howell's trying to get me," Paul said.

In a breaking, panicked voice, Howell told him that GPS traced through the computer call showed that Kate's phone was just a few miles north of the Talmadge Bridge. It appeared to be stationary just off of the highway.

"Kate's phone is in South Carolina," Paul told Armstrong. "Since her car's here that means she's in another vehicle, and across state lines. There's no car here, so that means Miller must have her."

"I'm calling the FBI," Armstrong said. "You keep your friend glued to that GPS."

28. Chevy on the Levee

The Chevy sat motionless on a grass covered trail along a marsh embankment not far off U.S. Highway 17. Frank Miller fumbled with a strand of barbed wire that held together a few stakes which formed a crude gate across the path. He cursed when a spike nicked his forefinger and threw back the contraption just enough to get his car through.

In darkness they traveled slowly along ancient berms, dikes that intertwined trough the rice fields of 18th-century plantations, fields now mostly reclaimed by tidal marsh and forest. Finally, now a few miles from the highway, they were deep inside a vast expanse of reeds and tidal floods.

The car stopped. Kate noticed that there now was no connection for her cell phone, the nearest tower being miles away. After a few seconds, the trunk lid swung open, and Frank Miller loomed over her.

"Get out," he said, holding the Ruger over her.

Kate felt frozen with shock, as well as pain, and couldn't move her legs enough to change her position. Just then, she found a new source of leverage in her hips and turned them, so they were flat on the bed of the trunk. She raised her arm weakly.

"Help me. I can't move."

When Frank grudgingly reached out with his left hand to grasp her wrist, she raised her hips a few inches, then slammed them back down as she kicked her legs straight up, striking Miller hard in the face with her left foot. He fell stumbling back, the gun falling just over the edge of the berm but not down the embankment.

Kate vaulted her shoulders over the back of the car, hit the ground hard but was up in an instant and running madly down the berm in the direction from which they had come. She heard the car start behind her and looked back just in time to see Miller backing rapidly toward her, but he lost control and ran the left tire over the bank.

She took another breath and started running again, hearing Miller's loud curses behind her. Fifty yards away she heard the whiz of a round just past her head and the crack of the pistol. She had come to a point where the dike split off into a stretch of sand on some higher though unstable ground in the marsh. In the light of the moon emerging from an opening in the cloudy sky, Kate could see water and heard the ripple of waves. She realized that there was a sandbar ahead and ran in that direction. She looked back after about 30 yards and saw another muzzle flash. The bullet splatted into the mud ahead of her.

She scrambled down another embankment, lying as flat as she could against it, practically rolling herself along while struggling to keep from sliding into the creek bed below. The tide was rushing in, and slippery clusters of oyster beds lay just at the water line. Once she slid and a shell sliced through the bottom of her tennis shoe and into her foot. She heard the sound of the gun again but saw nothing but darkness as the moon retreated once more behind black clouds.

Then she heard the sound of a helicopter.

A chopper took off at 10:37 p.m. from the Beaufort Marine Corps Air Station carrying F.B.I. agent Thomas Smalls, who minutes earlier had received a call about a kidnapping in Savannah. The pilot, Staff Sgt. Demarcus Greaves, aimed for the coordinates relayed by Howell Barker through the Savannah Police pinpointing the location where Kate's phone finally lost its connection. Beside Greaves was Lance Cpl. Clarence Higgins, a Marine marksman carrying an M16 with laser scope and infrared goggles just in case he wound up needing them. Smalls sat just behind them.

They saw the flashes of the pistol shots through the marsh. It was very near their location but off to the right, so Greaves angled the ship that way. He turned on the search light and flew low enough over the marsh grass that it swayed in the wind from the rotor blades but high enough to keep the target in clear sight.

Smalls thought he saw something just beyond the edge of the light beam, so Greaves ascended to 200 feet to cast a wider arc and they saw the muddied Kate clinging to the side of the bank, with the turning tide already lapping at her feet. He turned the light back a bit and there was Miller, pointing the weapon toward Kate as if he was about to fire another shot.

As the searchlight turned fully on him, Miller lifted his gun toward the helicopter and fired two shots at the maddening, blinding light that showered him. Corporal Higgins raised his rifle and fired once. The bullet entered just above the left clavicle and burst out Miller's back, leaving the arm dangling as his body twisted and convulsed violently and in a mighty spasm tumbled into the creek.

29. Lights in the Dark

Kate felt like she was hanging only by her tendons as she clung to a bulwark of sand and marine clay built into an ancient oyster bed. Shells still pricked her feet, although she put as little pressure on them as possible. She used her fingers to dig into the bank as much as she could, while cold saltwater swirled above her waist. She knew she'd suffer hypothermia and drown if she stayed put.

By now, Kate was very near the end of the dike where it rose prominently in the midst of the marsh, apparently part of an ancient pine hammock washed by tidal storms for centuries. By the moonlight which faded in and out through rapid clouds she spied a coquina stone outcropping a few feet away, at a level just above her head. If she could get close enough, she thought she could pull herself up and out of the water.

The helicopter whirled above. The pilot turned a light on Kate and Special Agent Small's voice bellowed: "Hang on, miss! This is the FBI. We're coming for you! The pilot is unsure about landing. We're sending someone down to assist."

Those words — and the light fixed on the ledge — gave Kate the spark she needed. With every minute bit of energy remaining and every iota of willpower left she began edging toward higher ground, hugging the slippery surface, and thrusting toes into the muddy shell cluster. With every slip, she advanced a tiny step or two and slowly moved close enough to get her hands on the rock.

Corporal Higgins was lowered on a rope ladder equipped with a sling to carry people out of tight spots. He darted to the edge of the berm and could see Kate pulling herself onto the ledge about five feet below him. She was out of the water but shivering fiercely, in sure danger of hypothermia. He shouted, "Look up!," and as she gazed vacantly at him, "I'm tossing you my jacket. You need to keep warm." He tossed her his wool-lined Navy windbreaker, which she managed to clutch and immediately wrap around her arms and shoulders.

The Marine's radio crackled on. "I might need some help. I can get down there to reach her, but she's not going to help much getting herself up."

"Help is on the way, Life Flight included," pilot Greaves responded. "Wind's picking up. That's not going to help anybody, especially not with those soft embankments around such a narrow zone."

Kate was feeling weaker by the second. Twice she thought she was about to pass out and fall. Miraculously, she held on.

"Now, what the hell is that?" she heard the corporal say.

A light, just a tiny speck at first, appeared in the distance. It flickered and bounced, vanished briefly, then returned appearing noticeably closer, turned slightly to the northeast, disappeared again, then reappeared coming directly on but shaking and wobbling, like a drunk with a flashlight trying to run across a field in the dark.

"We're having to pull up. Surface winds are becoming vicious," the pilot broadcast over the PA. "I'm going around to come around and back in at a better angle."

As the chopper maneuvered quickly up and away, Kate heard a growling motor sound. "Halt or I'll shoot," Higgins ordered through a megaphone. "Identify yourself!"

"Paul Camden!" came a reply muffled by the wind and the fading sound of the helicopter.

"Paul!" Kate screamed.

Realizing she knew him, the corporal allowed Paul to advance. With a short burst of his bike, he was at the end of the dike. Seeing his face, life and hope returned to her eyes.

"Don't try to talk, baby. Save your strength to get out of here."

Paul turned to Higgins. "What's your plan?"

"The only way I see to do it," the corporal replied, "is to get down below her and push up as well as pull. I think she's too weak to get a grip otherwise.

"I was going to take a line and dive in, climb up and tie it around her, then get the skipper to pull us up to solid ground. But since you're here..."

Paul nodded approvingly. "Tie me up. Just another minute, baby!"

As they looped the rope around Paul's shoulders and waist, Higgins asked, "Mind telling me how you got out here? I'm curious cause I ride myself and I'll be damned if I can figure how you navigated this."

Paul shook his head. "The miracle is that it started at all. When it did, I just rode. I rode to the point where we figured the car had turned off the highway and followed the trail. For the most part I followed the only logical way to go. Twice it could go either way. Once I got it right and once I had to jump a creek to get back on track. But I'm here."

"Let's pray your luck continues," the corporal said, tightening the cinch.

Paul took one last look at the dark foamy brine and jumped. Higgins held fast to the other end of the line.

Kate saw Paul's head surface just a few feet away. She could tell the tide was fierce now because he had to swim quickly beside her. With his boots it was easier to get a toehold, and with Higgins tugging on the rope he was quickly beside her on the rock.

Rather than try to tie her, he looped the line under her arms and held her while the Marine pulled, and Paul kicked his way the few feet up.

As they reached the top and collapsed on the matted marsh grasses, the Marine helicopter was returning, and Life Flight was approaching. Other lights in the distance signaled efforts to converge on the scene by boat and what little land there was.

"I thought you'd never get here," Kate said.

"I was afraid I'd never see you alive again."

He kissed her and rose to his feet. Frank Miller's body suddenly emerged, rolling over in a thatch of reeds churning in the creek. His one remaining arm pointed skyward, and then he was submerged again, soon to be carried towards the islands and the sea, perhaps never to be seen again, his family history and all the city's history that he knew vanishing with him.

Exhaustion finally overtook her, and Kate fell unconscious.

30. Investigation Over

When Kate awoke it was raining and water trickled down her hospital room window in time with the drip into her veins. She could see nothing else but a funereal gray sky. It took her a moment to realize where she was, and when she did her mind automatically began taking inventory of the pain.

Her foot was numb in a way that is typical of an injury moderated by heavy medication. She seemed to be wrapped in gauze from head to toe but assumed if anything was broken there would be a cast or splint somewhere. Still, despite the drugs coursing through her body, she ached all over.

"Candler Hospital," Kate thought to herself as the grogginess subsided and the meaning of her surroundings and condition became clear. She began to remember now – soaking wet and freezing cold, the downdraft of the helicopter penetrating like it came from an ice tunnel. She recalled voices and strong arms lifting her from the churning muddy tidal flow and up the slippery embankment.

Paul, and someone else she believed, had hoisted her into the back of a chopper. The memory began to return the pain in her arms, legs and especially her wounded foot. She recalled Frank Miller's body bobbing in the swirling debris in the creek. She could hear the pilot radioing for instructions on where to carry her and calling in directions for local law enforcement to come secure the crime scene and try to retrieve Frank's corpse. Then she passed out.

Kate dozed for what seemed like a long time, dreaming of lazy summer evenings when the sun finally kneels, and the light falls evenly across the front porch. She dreamed of herself and Paul, aged and sitting in rocking chairs, with small children playing on the steps and joyous laughter from family members all around.

When she opened her eyes again, Paul was slumped in a chair by the bed, his eyelids quivering and knee twitching as though he was wrestling demons in a deep sleep.

She closed her eyes again, and in a few minutes he spoke.

"Kate." He was standing over her now, stroking the side of her head.

She smiled. "So, you were right all along. Only a real cuckoo bird would hatch a plot like that."

Relieved to see her awake and stronger than he expected, Paul reached for her hand.

"Yeah, when a crime makes no sense, you can bet an irrational mind is involved."

Kate squeezed his hand. "But you figured it out." She tried to wink and wound up furrowing her brow.

"Just in the nick of time. My God, he almost killed you while I was still fooling around. In all the years I've known him I never imagined he was capable of anything like that."

"No one did," Kate said. "It's not your fault."

"It's just that I should have known about his family history, Kate. It would have made solving this thing a whole lot easier."

"Let me get this straight. You're saying that if you knew Frank was Rosenkrantz's great grandson you would have figured out, he had the brains and the balls to kill people just to avenge a century old injustice against his family? And who would have come up with the idea of stashing their bodies in the parks, just on the thinnest thread of relevance to the Seraphim Society in the first place?"

Paul nodded. "But at least we would have been aware, and you never would have gone over there in the first place."

That thought sank in for a moment.

"They found the last victim's former lover in another crate at

Frank's house. According to Howell, Frank had been in love with her his entire life. She liked him, too, but had an inner desire to marry up. She never did. Remained single with that weird off and on relationship with her lover until Frank somehow wormed his way back into their lives and killed them.

"After seeing how easy it was to make people disappear without detection, he must have hatched his scheme to take out as many of his antagonists as he could. And in a dramatic way."

"Just as we thought, the Orleans Square corpse was to skew the investigation," Kate said.

"And, just as I figured, the guy who was really eating at the killer's insides was Lindsey Weatherford – the symbol of the greed and hypocrisy that he hated with a passion. It drove him nuts. He was running out of time and had to take too many chances in order to get Lindsey."

There was a long silence. Then Paul somberly said, "I'm sorry Kate. I still can't get it out of my mind. I never should have let you go there. I don't know, you have the right to never even see me again."

The rain had subsided now, and darkness was filling the sky, with one stubborn beam of light entering the hospital room window and creating a golden glow on the wall behind him.

"My choice, eh?" she said. He nodded in agreement.

"Well then, I think I'll put in a stipulation that you can never leave me. How's that?"

Relief poured through him. He bent over and kissed her gently so as not to disturb the bandages.

"Just one thing," he said. "In the future, leave all investigations to me."

It hurt her to laugh, but she picked up a pillow and hit him in the head with it.

"Investigations are over, mister!"

Somehow, deep inside neither of them thought that was true.

About the Author

Rome Collier has been writing stories or one sort of another for most of his life. After a journalistic career that took him from Hilton Head Island to the Middle East, he has published four other novels: the science fiction mind-bender The Planet of Games, followed by The Planet of Dreams; C.S.A: The Centennial, an alternative history; and The Second Coming, religious philosophy. This is the Greenville, S.C., native's first venture into the mystery/thriller genre. Rome lives in Thunderbolt, Ga., with his wife, Geni, and their dog Brandy.

A Note from Rome

"I would like to thank the folks at Maudlin Pond Press, especially Ben Goggins and Lauren Clackum for their editing and artistic design skills and Cathy Sakas, who saw something in the story that we all want to share. Without them, I feel sure the book would never have been published. I also would like to thank my wife, Geni, and all my family members who had to deal with me from time to time as I fretted over the manuscript."

www.ingramcontent.com/pod-product-compliance
Lightning Source LLC
Chambersburg PA
CBHW070359200726
48294CB00003B/1001
* 9 7 8 1 9 5 9 5 6 3 1 3 6 *